Jennie Maria Bingham

The Life of the Seventh Earl of Shaftesbury

Jennie Maria Bingham

The Life of the Seventh Earl of Shaftesbury

ISBN/EAN: 9783337416416

Printed in Europe, USA, Canada, Australia, Japan

Cover: Foto ©Raphael Reischuk / pixelio.de

More available books at **www.hansebooks.com**

The Life of the Seventh Earl of Shaftesbury, K. G. 👁👁

BY

JENNIE M. BINGHAM

CINCINNATI: CURTS & JENNINGS
NEW YORK: EATON & MAINS
1899

Life of Lord Shaftesbury

Introduction

WHEN a man becomes so great as was the Earl of Shaftesbury, his name and fame are a part of the common heritage of the human race. Measured by what he did and what he was, this illustrious man deserved the encomium passed upon him by the Duke of Argyle when he said:

"MY LORDS AND GENTLEMEN,—All the great reforms of the past fifty years have been brought about, not by the Liberal party, nor by the Tory party, but by the labors of one man—the Earl of Shaftesbury."

How he accomplished these reforms, how he abolished child slavery in the mining regions of England, how he shortened the hours of labor in the factories and threw the broad shield of British law over the heads of hundreds of thousands of working people, is told with graphic power in this book.

Shaftesbury earned the right to say to every other reformer, "Let no one despair of a good cause for want of helpers. Let him persevere, *persevere*, PERSEVERE, and God will raise up friends and helpers."

The story of this wonderful life as here portrayed, should be placed in the hands of every boy and girl in the Republic. It would be "extravagant economy" to deny them the inspiration of the life of a man whose name is a household word in England, and should become so in America.

CHARLES C. McCABE.

Contents

5

The Life of Lord Shaftesbury

Chapter I

THE life-story of Anthony Ashley Cooper, the seventh Earl of Shaftesbury, is one of the rarest and most beautiful ever lived or written. Victor Hugo's "Good Bishop" in "Les Miserables" is said to be immortal, because he acted like Christ. In a far more enduring way will this noble nobleman, Lord Shaftesbury, take hold of coming centuries, because he, not as a novelist's creation, but as a real man, acted like Christ.

During a public life of over fifty years he

was identified with more organizations for the uplifting of humanity than any man who ever lived.

He literally gave up all to follow Christ. He resigned honors of state, luxuries of home, time for intellectual culture, and spent all his income to help the wretched and degraded. The lower down they were, the greater their claim to his service.

When he was urged to accept a place in the ministry of the realm, he replied:

"I can not satisfy myself that to accept office is a divine call; but I am satisfied that God has called me to labor among the poor."

A little later, when a position of high honor was offered, he said: "One million and six hundred thousand operatives are still excluded from the benefits of the factory acts, and so long as they are unprotected I can not take office."

He was very fond of literature and all branches of science, especially astronomy; never so happy as when he could spend his days in close application to books and instruments, and his nights in the observatory with the eminent astronomer, Sir James South, whose firm friend he was. He dared to hope that he, too, might become an astronomer.

But the duties of his life-work began to press upon him. His visits to the observatory became less frequent until they ceased altogether. He says of himself at last:

"I was called to another career, and now I find myself, at the end of a long life, not a philosopher, not an author, but simply an old man who has endeavored to do his duty."

He did not receive the inspiration for his life of beautiful service from his parents, but from a humble servant who was housekeeper in the family. She formed a strong attachment for the gentle, serious child, and would take him in her arms and tell him the sweet story of the Manger of Bethlehem and the Cross of Calvary.

Although not yet seven years old, there was in his heart a distinct longing to be Christ-like, which ultimately developed into an intelligent faith. She taught him a prayer—the first he had ever learned, and which he never omitted to use in the trying days so soon to follow. When an old man, he often found himself repeating those simple words.

"The greatest man that England has ever produced," says one, "was this Ashley Cooper, Earl of Shaftesbury, and he was brought to Christ by a humble, unlettered servant girl."

This lowly handmaid little knew that generations unknown and years untold would rise up to bless her. He delighted to honor her memory, and the watch which she left him was the only one he ever carried. He was fond of showing it, and would say, "This was given to me by Maria Millis, the best friend I ever had."

His father was absorbed in business, and his mother gave all of her attention to the gay life of the society about her. It is evident that Lord Ashley and his brothers and sisters experienced unkindness, almost amounting to cruelty, from both parents, when they were young, but especially from the mother. They were aristocratic and worldly in the extreme.

When only seven years old he was sent to school at Chiswick. In later years he said:

"The memory of that place makes me shudder. I think there was never such a wicked school before or since; the treatment was bullying, starvation, and cruelty."

Here he lived in a state of constant terror from the cruelty of the elder boys, and suffered exquisite misery for years through the neglect of the teacher to provide the necessities of life. Dickens, in "Nicholas Nickleby," has shown us the sort of schools which existed at the beginning of this century. They were hotbeds of every kind of evil and mischief, where might was right, and weak and timid boys suffered intolerably. He knew what it was to shiver with cold through the long nights, and to be pinched with starvation.

It was noticed in Lord Shaftesbury that a certain sadness surrounded him like an atmosphere. It was, no doubt, in a measure due to the scenes of suffering and sorrow which were constantly before him. But it was also attributable to the fact that there had been no lightheartedness in his childhood. His biographer suggests that in these years he was graduating for his life-work. He had known what it was to be oppressed, lonely, suffering, hungry; henceforth he would plead the cause of the oppressed and suffering, and bring joy and gladness to the hearts of little children.

His first great grief came at a time when he was least able to bear it. Maria Millis, the only grown-up person in the world whom he loved, and the only one who had ever sympathized with his simple child-faith, was called to her rest. He felt that his last chance of happiness had gone. Without a soul on earth to whom he could go for comfort, he turned to the old Book that she had loved, and spread his sorrows before the Heavenly Friend whom she had taught him to regard as full of pity and tenderness.

At about sixteen he went to live with a
clergyman, distantly related. He was sent
there, in fact, to be got out of the way; for the
clergyman never professed to teach him anything.

Lord Ashley's father determined to put
him into the army; but a friend of whom Ashley spoke with the deepest gratitude, per-
suaded the father to send him to Oxford University instead.

Here he had a fine tutor, whose first question proved to be a stimulus to the young
fellow. It was, "Do you intend to take a
degree?"

This was a strong demand on one who had
lost so many years, but he answered, "I will
try." He *did* try, and the result was that he
led in classics. Referring to this in after-life,
he said, modestly:

"I have had a great many surprises in my
life; but I do not think I was ever more surprised than when I took honors at Oxford."

He could remember the day and hour in

which he determined upon a philanthropic
career. It was when a schoolboy of fourteen,
he was one day walking down Harrow Hill,
and was startled by hearing a great shouting,
and the singing of a low, drinking song. Presently the noisy party turned the street corner,
and to his horror he saw that four or five
drunken men were carrying a roughly-made
coffin containing the body of one of their fellows for burial. No solitary soul was there
as a mourner. A fellow-creature was about
to be consigned to his grave with indignities
to which not even a dog should be subjected.
Young Ashley exclaimed, "Can this be permitted simply because the man was poor and
friendless!"

Before the sound of the drunken song had
died away, he had faced the future of his life,
and determined to make the cause of the poor
his own.

He wrote in his journal:

"Time was when I could not sleep for ambition. I thought of nothing but fame and

immortality. I could not bear the idea of dying and being forgotten. But now I am much changed. I desire only to be useful in my generation.

"I have been considering my future career. The first principle, God's honor; the second, man's happiness; the means, prayer and unremitting diligence."

He was all his life very sensitive to criticism, and had a nervous fear of failure, which made him shrink from every undertaking. When we think of the abuse to which he was subjected as he "went about doing good," we get a glimpse of the heroic spirit of the man.

His first appointment was on the India Board, and here he labored against sutteeism (the burning of the widow on the death of her husband). He was put down at once as a madman, and was told never to mention such a thing again, that the natives would murder the English if they passed a law against sutteeism.

But Lord Ashley would *not* be silenced until

this outrageous evil was abolished.   His next
effort was to introduce horticulture into India.
He wisely argued that the introduction of
choice vegetables and potatoes into India
would not only become a resource in calam-
itous times, but would bring about a more
friendly feeling between the natives and Eu-
ropeans.

In his journal he says:

"India, what can I do for your countless
myriads?   There are two things—good government and Christianity!   O God, tip my
tongue with fire!"

Chapter II

IN 1830 occurred an event of great importance relating to Lord Ashley's private life.
He had written a year before:

"If I could find the creature I have invented, I should love her with a tenderness
and truth unprecedented in the history of
wedlock. I pray for her abundantly. God
grant me this purest of blessings!"

That prayer had been answered; and on
the 10th of June, 1830, he was married to
Emily, daughter of the fifth Earl Cowper.
For forty years she shared her husband's
struggles, inspired his efforts, and was, as he
himself has described her, "a wife as true, as
good, and as deeply beloved as God ever gave
to man."

Referring to this period of Lord Ashley's
life, Lord Granville, who had known him from
boyhood, says:

"He was a singularly fine-looking man.

He had that striking presence and those manly good looks which, I believe, help a man more than we sometimes think, and they helped him when he endeavored to inspire his humble fellow-countrymen with his noble nature. Those good looks he retained to the end of his life. At the time I am speaking of, he was about to marry that bright and beautiful woman who afterward threw so much sunshine on his home."

On the anniversary of his wedding-day, Lord Ashley wrote in his journal:

"No man, I am sure, ever enjoyed more happiness in his married life. God be praised! Were I not married to a woman whose happiness, even for an hour, I prefer to whole years of my own, I could wish to be carried away from this scene of destruction, rather than see my country crumble before my eyes."

Lord Ashley entered so thoroughly into the sorrows of life, that the delights of home companionship were necessary to keep him from despondency. He was often in utter

despair over his public work, and he needed
a wife who believed in him, and who believed
in all that he hoped. When he was asked to
enter the House of Commons, and knew that
it meant a political career, the expenses of
which would be very heavy for his slender
income, and the trials of which would make
it a thorny path, he wanted to turn back to
private life. Robert Southey, his friend, advised him so to do; but to turn back meant
that he must give up the reforms which
he was hoping to establish, and which he
knew must be advocated in the Houses of
Parliament.

His first important speech in Parliament
was on behalf of the most unfortunate, the
most wretched, and the most ill-treated of his
fellow-creatures—the pauper lunatics of London. In it he sounded the keynote of his
whole Parliamentary career. From that day
forward his whole life was devoted to the great
interests of humanity.

In the early part of this century, lunatics

had passed the period of being canonized as
saints, burnt as heretics, or hanged as criminals. If only suspected of being dangerous,
society, in terror, took the most cruel precau-
tions for its own safety, with an utter disre-
gard for the feelings of the unfortunates, or
for their chances of recovery. Lunatics were
kept constantly chained to walls in dark cells,
and had nothing to lie upon but straw. The
keepers visited them, whip in hand, and lashed
them into obedience. They were half-
drowned in "baths of surprise," and in some
cases semi-strangulation was resorted to. The
"baths of surprise" were so constructed that
the patients in passing over a trap-door fell
in. Some patients were chained in wells, and
the water made to rise until it reached their
chins. One horrible contrivance was a rotary
chair, in which patients were made to sit and
were revolved at a frightful speed. Women
as well as men were flogged, chained to iron
bars, and confined to iron cages. Londoners
out for a holiday paid their twopences to stroll

through Bedlam and laugh at the poor lunatics.

The only act of Parliament providing for the care of pauper lunatics, authorized any two justices to apprehend them, and have them locked up and chained. Any one who chose, could get a license to keep an asylum, and though the College of Physicians could receive reports of abuses, they could do nothing further.

The Society of Friends had started at York a "Retreat" for insane members of their society. Attention was drawn to this enlightened experiment, and at the same time to the frightful abuses at a large asylum in the same city. A committee was appointed, and a bill for the investigation of madhouses was passed by the House of Commons, but was thrown out by the House of Lords. The old idea that connected madness with evil spirits, and made the safety of the community the only matter of consideration, was long in giving place to sounder views. -

This was the state of things when Lord
Ashley made his first speech in Parliament.
He spoke in favor of a bill which provided for
the appointment of fifteen commissioners, and
the requirement of two medical certificates for
patients. Lord Ashley was one of the commissioners appointed. In the following year
he became chairman of the Commission, and
continued in that office till his death, a period
of fifty-seven years, his great interest in the
welfare of the insane having been sustained
throughout that long period with unflagging
energy. Afterward, when the commissioners
were salaried, he remained the unpaid chairman.

Nothing of striking importance was accomplished for several years. During this period,
Lord Ashley did not leave a stone unturned
which could be of assistance to the contem-
plated reform. He visited the asylums in
London and the provinces, and saw the filthy
condition, the horrible attendant circumstances, the misery and degradation of the in-

mates. He saw for himself that the lunatics
were chained to their beds, and left from Sat-
urday afternoon till Monday without attendance, and with only bread and water within
their reach. He saw that the violent and the
quiet, the clean and the uncleanly, were shut
up together in foul and disgusting cells. But
what astonished him more than anything else
was, that people knew and cared absolutely
nothing about it. So shocked and horrified
was he with the revelation of misery and cruelty that he vowed he would never cease
pleading the cause of these poor creatures till
either death silenced him or the laws were
amended. And, as we shall see, he kept his
vow.

A record in his journal says:

"Yesterday I spent with our Lunatic Commission. There is nothing poetical in this
duty; but every sigh prevented and every pang
subdued is a song of harmony to the heart. I
have chosen political life, because I have, by
God's blessing, many advantages of birth and

situation which, although of trifling value if unsupported, are yet very powerful aids if joined to zeal and honesty."

Political papers derisively called him "the Lunatic's Friend."

It has been well said that the services which Lord Ashley rendered to this cause alone would have carried his name down to posterity in the front rank of English philanthropists.

This extract from one of his speeches shows us how he sought to lay this matter on the hearts of his hearers:

"These unhappy persons are outcasts from all the social and domestic affections of private life, and have no refuge but in the laws. You can prevent by the agency you shall appoint the recurrence of frightful cruelties. You can soothe the days of the incurable, and restore many sufferers to health and usefulness. For we must not run away with the notion that even the hopelessly mad are dead to all capacity of intellectual or moral exer-

tion. Quite the reverse; their feelings, too,
are painfully alive. I have seen them writhe
under supposed contempt, while a word of
kindness and respect would kindle their whole
countenance into an expression of joy. Their
condition appeals to our highest sympathies.
I trust that I shall stand excused for having
consumed so much of your valuable time,
when you call to mind that the motion is made
on behalf of the most helpless, if not the most
afflicted, portion of the human race."

He cited the case of a lady who had been
shut up as a lunatic, but, as far as he and three
other commissioners could judge, she was as
sane as any woman in England. He spared no
pains in sifting the evidence on both sides,
and prosecuted the investigation day by day
until he had proof indisputable that the lady
was the victim of a cruel conspiracy, and was
perfectly sane. She was, of course, set at liberty with the least possible delay.

He narrated an anecdote to show that eminent men sometimes formed their opinions as

to the sanity of a patient on very flimsy evidence. Once, when he was sitting on the Commission as chairman, the alleged insanity of a lady was under discussion, and he took a view of the case opposite to that of his colleagues. One of the medical men who was there to give evidence crept up to his chair, and in a confidential tone said, "Are you aware, my lord, that she subscribes to the Society for the Conversion of the Jews?" "Indeed," replied Lord Ashley, "and are you aware that I am president of that society?"

One story out of many, illustrating the characteristic promptness with which, even late in life, he would examine a case and take immediate action, may be given here:

A lady, Mrs. A——, was on visiting terms with Mrs. B——, a woman of fashion and position. There was very little in common between the two, and the visits of Mrs. A—— would have been less frequent than they were, had she not taken a more than passing interest in a charming young lady who was living in

the home of Mrs. B——. One day when Mrs.
A—— called, Miss C—— was not there, and
on making very pointed inquiries, she was,
after some hesitation, informed that her young
friend was out of her mind, and was in an
asylum fifty miles out of town. Mrs. A——
felt troubled and distressed. She had seen
Miss C—— only a week before, and perceived
no indication of a disordered mind. At length
it occurred to her that Lord Shaftesbury was
a commissioner in lunacy, and she went
straight to his house, found him at home, and
told him the whole story. It was evening
when she arrived in Grosvenor Square, and
dinner was on the table; but within a quarter
of an hour Lord Shaftesbury was on his way to
the railway station to go down to the asylum
and investigate the matter for himself. He
did so, and on the following day the young
lady was released, it having been authorita-
tively stated that she was not insane.

In his seventy-sixth year, his portrait was
painted by the famous artist, Sir John Millais.

The *Times*, in its art critique, said:

"These worn lines in the face of the great philanthropist would be painful were they not pathetic."

About this time he wrote in his journal:

"Beyond the circle of my own commissioners and the lunatics that I visit, not a soul in great or small life has had any notion of the years of toil and care that, under God, I have bestowed on this melancholy and awful question."

The year before he died, the commissioners of lunacy were attacked in the House of Lords, and it looked for a time as if Lord Shaftesbury's work would be overturned. Very pathetic are the outpourings of his heart as he contemplates the possibility of the labor, the toils, the anxieties, the prayers of more than fifty years being in one moment brought to naught. After a few weeks, the bill against the commissioners was shelved, and Shaftesbury remained with the great work which he had carried on to such blessed success.

Chapter III

IT was when Lord Ashley was beginning his public career that attention was called to the position of the workingman. His only resource was self-defense, his only argument was violence. Education was at a deplorably low ebb. It was found that a factory district with over one hundred thousand population did not have one public day-school for poor children. The amusements of the people were a fair index of their general condition. There was universal rioting and carousal at Easter; drunkenness was the great prevailing vice; unchastity was fearfully prevalent, and low-class dancing saloons, and still lower-class cheap theaters were largely frequented. The factory system, as we shall presently see, was cruel in its oppression. Mines and collieries were worked in great measure by women and children. Sanitary science was practically un-

known. Ragged schools, reformatory and industrial schools, and workmen's clubs had not
begun to exist. The newspaper was fettered.
Taxation was oppressive and unjust. The
poor laws were pauperizing and degrading.
The cheap literature reflected the violent pas-
sions which raged on every side, and the
Church was in a state of lethargy from which
it was not effectually aroused for many years.

In 1829, Sir Robert Peel's Act laid the
foundation for the present police force. Before that time the public were dependent for
their protection upon a staff of parochial
watchmen, who were muffled up in heavy
cloaks, and beat a stick upon the pavement to
announce their approach, and allow evil-dis-
posed persons to get out of their way. At
night they carried lanterns, which served, as
the stick by day, to announce their where-
abouts, and after they had made their rounds
they retired to their watch-boxes. Robbery of
all kinds was committed with impunity, and

after sunset it was not safe to venture on the street.

Strangely enough, the Robert Peel Act met with fiercest opposition and invective. It was considered an interference with personal liberty and a menace to public peace. The popular prejudice yielded when it was found the best protection for life and property.

It was fortunate for Lord Ashley that the police force should have been instituted at this period. It would have been impossible for him to get personally acquainted with the dens of infamy and the abominations in the hovels of the lowest of the low, without the assistance of the police, a body of men to whom he always acknowledged his indebtedness.

In 1833 the great work of factory legislation began, in which for twenty years Lord Ashley was to take so prominent a part.

Machinery was invented which children could manage almost as well as adults. A demand for child-labor was created, and it was supplied in a manner which scarcely seems credible to the humanity of to-day. Large numbers of children were drafted from the workhouses of London, Edinburgh, and other great cities, and placed in the mills as "apprentices," where, at the discretion of sordid overseers, they were worked unmercifully and brutally treated. Voices had been raised in protest against the cruel wrongs inflicted on these poor children, who were continually being sent down to Lancashire by barge-loads from the London workhouses. But in the excitement of stirring events, which were then occurring at home and abroad, those voices were unheeded.

Meantime, the condition of these unfortunate children was growing so bad, that the cruelty of the system under which they were held was hardly paralleled by the abominations of Negro slavery. A horrible traffic had sprung up; child jobbers scoured the country for the purpose of purchasing children, to sell them again into the bondage of factory slaves.

The waste of human life in the factories to which the children were consigned was simply frightful. Day and night the machinery was kept going, one gang of children working it by day and another set by night, while in times of pressure the same children were kept working day and night by remorseless taskmasters.

Under the "apprentice system" bargains were made between the churchwardens and overseers of parishes and the owners of factories, whereby pauper children, some as young as five years old, were bound to serve until they were twenty-one.

In some cases alluring promises were made to them. They were told they would be well clothed and fed, have plenty of money, and learn a trade. These deceptions were practiced in order to make the children wish to go, and thus give an opportunity to the traffickers to say that they went voluntarily.

Their first labors consisted in picking up loose cotton from the floor. This they did amidst the din of machinery in a burning at-

3

mosphere laden with fumes of the oil with which the axles of twenty thousand wheels and spindles were bathed.

With aching backs and ankles inflamed from the constant stooping, with fingers lacerated from scraping the floors, parched and suffocated by dust, the little slaves toiled from morning till night. If they paused, the brutal overseer, who was responsible for a certain amount of work being performed by each child under him, urged them on by kicks and blows.

When the dinner-time came after six hours labor, it was only to rest for forty minutes and eat black bread and porridge. As they grew older, employment involving longer hours and harder work was given to them. Lost time had to be made up by overwork, and they were required every other day to spend the dinner-hour cleaning the frames. They sank into the profoundest depths of wretchedness. In weariness they often fell upon the machinery, and almost every factory child was more or less injured.

There was no redress of any kind. The isolation of the mills aided to conceal the cruelties. The children could not escape, as rewards were offered for their capture, and were eagerly sought. They could not complain when the visiting magistrate came, for they were in abject fear of their taskmasters. If they perished in the machinery, it was a rare thing for a coroner's inquest to be held.

When their indentures expired, after years of toil averaging fourteen hours a day, with their bodies scarred with the wounds inflicted by the overseers, with their minds dwarfed and vacant, with their constitutions injured, these unfortunate apprentices arrived at manhood, to find that they had never been taught the trade they should have learned, and that they had no resource whatever but to enter again upon the hateful life from which they were at last legally freed. If they had become crippled or diseased during their apprenticeship, their wages were fixed at the lowest possible sum.

Some laws had been passed against the apprentice system, and limiting the hours of labor for children, but all this applied to cotton factories only, and the abuses in woolen, linen, and silk factories were as great. Then a Mr. Sadler introduced his famous "Ten-hour Bill" in the House of Commons; but he was violently opposed, and finally not returned to Parliament. Then the poor mill-hands felt that the death-blow had been struck to all their interests.

It was then that Lord Ashley, who had supported the Ten-hour Bill, was asked to take up the cause of the factory people. On the one hand lay ease, influence, promotion, and troops of friends; on the other, the most unpopular question of the day, unceasing labor amidst every kind of opposition, perpetual anxiety, estrangement of friends, and a life among the poor. It was between these he had to choose.

Had he been ambitious of political distinction, his abilities, his popularity, and his great oratorical powers would have commanded a prominent position in his party. Already he had won an appointment in the Government under the Duke of Wellington, whose confidence he enjoyed, and whose approbation he had won.

But Lord Ashley was not a man to be influenced by these considerations. "Already he had passed through the strait gate of his path in life, and had entered the narrow way." He remembered that day at Harrow when he vowed that he would fight against the monstrous cruelty that allowed the weak to be trampled upon, simply because they were poor.

But that vow had been made when he was a mere boy. Now he had a wife and a child, a home and a position. To espouse the factory cause was to give up home comfort and domestic leisure, to relinquish scientific and literary pursuits.

He laid the matter before his wife, painted in dark colors all the sacrifice it meant for her, and waited for her verdict. "It is your duty to

go forward," she said, "and the consequences
we must leave."

It was characteristic of Lord Ashley that
he did not wish to receive more than his share
of credit.   Later in life, when his speeches on
this subject were published, he wrote:

"I desire to record the invaluable services
of the remarkable men who preceded me.
Had they not gone before and borne such an
amount of responsibility and toil, I do not
believe that it would have been in my power
to have achieved anything at all."

Lord Ashley had made it a principle at the
outset of his career, not to advocate any cause
until he had acquainted himself with all the
facts by close personal investigation.   "I made
it an invariable rule," he said, "to see everything with my own eyes, to take nothing on
trust or hearsay.   In factories I examined the
mills, the machinery, the homes, and saw the
work and workers.   In collieries I went down
into the pits.   In London I went into lodging-
houses, and thieves' haunts, and every filthy

place. It gave me a power I could not otherwise have had. I could speak of things from actual experience, and I used often to hear things from the poor sufferers themselves which were invaluable to me. I got to know their habits of thought and action and their actual wants. I sat, and had tea and talk with them hundreds of times."

When the Committee of Investigation was in Manchester, the entire company of child operatives marched in a body to the hotel. These men had never looked upon such a procession before — three thousand ragged, wretched little ones, attended by at least fifteen thousand spectators. It was an argument of overwhelming force.

Robert Southey wrote Lord Ashley, begging him not to go to the manufacturing districts any more. He said: "The distressful recollections will be impressed upon you, and burnt in, and your health will be affected seriously thereby."

Southey did not know that the whole pathway of his friend's life would lie through scenes of suffering "burnt in," which need not have been his lot if he had not dedicated himself to the poor and friendless.

In a speech at Leeds, Lord Ashley instanced the case of a young woman in a mill at Stockport, who had been caught by the machinery, whirled around, and dashed to the ground, with limbs broken and body mutilated. Her employers deducted eighteen pence from her wages for the remainder of the week after the accident happened! Lord Ashley prosecuted the mill-owners, with the result that they had to pay £100 damages to the girl, and expenses on both sides, amounting to £600. He showed them that the expenditure of a few shillings in properly boxing the machinery would have saved the financial loss to the mill-owners, and the more terrible loss to the injured girl.

In a speech he called attention to some boys who were made to work for thirty-four hours successively in the foul cellar of a York-

shire factory, the air of which was so bad that
workmen tied handkerchiefs around their faces
before going into the place. He reminded the
House that when, in its wisdom and mercy, it
decided that forty-five hours in a week was a
term of labor long enough for an adult Negro,
it would not now be unbecoming to consider
whether sixty-nine hours a week were not too
many for the children of the British Empire.

Just when factory legislation became the
burning question of the day, and it looked as
though Lord Ashley would win his cause, an
endeavor was made to thwart him from another standpoint. He was offered a position
in the Government where it would be impossible for him to carry on a great political agitation.

The pretext was made that his "high morality" required his services in the royal household. Sir Robert Peel, who planned the
scheme, did not know the man with whom he
had to deal. He was incapable of realizing
the high and generous motives of one who, for

the sake of the poor and oppressed, was ready
to sacrifice position and emolument, and close
upon himself the gates leading to political
power.

This was his reply: "There are still 1,600,-
000 operatives excluded from the benefits of
the Factory Acts; until they are brought
under the protection of the law, I can not take
office."

Later, in speaking of the obstacles which
beset him at this period, he said:

"I had to break every political connection,
to encounter a most formidable array of cap-
italists, mill-owners, and men who, by natural
impulse, hate all 'humanity mongers.' They
easily influence the ignorant, the timid, and
the indifferent."

A record in his journal shows the spirit
with which he worked:

"Addressed a body of operatives last night.
Admirable meeting. Urged the most concili-
atory sentiments towards employers. Urged,
too, the indispensable necessity of private and

public prayer if they desire to accomplish their end. Told what I felt, that unless the Spirit of Christ had commanded my service, I would not have undertaken the task. It was to *religion* therefore, and not to *me*, that they were indebted for benefits received. What a place is Manchester—silent and solemn; the rumble of carriages and groaning of mills, but few voices and no merriment. Intensely occupied in the production of material wealth, it regards that alone as the grand end of human existence. Thirty-five thousand children, under thirteen years of age, many not exceeding five or six, are worked at times for fifteen hours a day! O blessed Lord and Savior of mankind, look down on these lambs of thy fold, and strengthen me for this service!"

There were times when the outcome of his cause looked dark. This appears most pathetically in his journal:

"Twelve years of labor, anxiety, and responsibility! I have borrowed and spent in reference to .my income enormous sums of

money, and am shut out from every hope of
emolument and path of honorable ambition.
My own kinsfolk dislike my opinions, and per-
secute me. I am excluded from my father's
house because I have maintained the cause of
the laborer. It has been toil by day and by
night, fears and disappointments, prayers and
tears, long journeys and unceasing letters."

It was not until Lord Ashley had given
fourteen years of such service that his bill was
passed, and received the royal assent. This
great victory was received throughout the
country with intense enthusiasm. The rejoic-
ing in the manufacturing districts was such as
had never been seen before. Lord Ashley was
greeted with ovations wherever he went.
Medals were struck in commemoration of the
event, one of which was sent to the Queen
from the operatives by the hand of Lord Ashley. His record of this event says: "I can find
neither breath nor sense to express my joy.
Praised be the Lord! Praised be the Lord!"

The bill limited the time of children to six

hours a day. There was protection against accident, death, or mutilation from the un-guarded state of machinery, and the provision that no woman should work over twelve hours a day. Buildings must be kept clean. Children must not clean machinery while in mo-tion. A certain number of holidays were im-posed. The children must go to school, and the employer must have a certificate to that effect.

Lord Ashley's perseverance brought over to his side many of those who had bitterly opposed him. One who had been particularly hostile stood forth in Parliament, and made his public recantation. He said:

"Very early in my Parliamentary career, Lord Ashley, now the Earl of Shaftesbury, in-troduced a bill of this description. I opposed him, and was very much influenced in my op-position by what the manufacturers said. They declared that it was the last half-hour of the work performed by their operatives which made all their profits, and if we took away that last half-hour, we would ruin the manufacturers of England. I listened to that statement, and trembled for the manufacturers; but Lord Ashley persevered. Parliament passed the bill which he brought in. From that time down to the present the factories of this country have been under State control, and I appeal to this House whether the manufacturers of England have suffered by this legislation."

This was greeted by loud cheering. It was officially declared that factory legislation had consolidated society, swept away a great mass of festering discontent, and placed the prosperity of the district on a safe, educated, contented basis.

In 1860, on an August day, about four thousand persons assembled in the Free Trade Hall at Manchester, to witness the presentation to the Countess of Shaftesbury of a fine marble bust of the noble Earl as a testimonial of the gratitude of the factory operatives.

The Countess, in acknowledging the presentation, said:

"My good friends, it will not require many words for me to express the deep and heartfelt gratitude with which I receive this testimonial. I prize it highly as coming from a large body of my countrymen, whose intelligence and morality qualifies them to estimate at their true value any efforts made for the welfare of the community. Having watched your exertions with lively interest, I warmly rejoiced in your success; and it is my fervent prayer to God that it may be blessed through many generations to you and your children."

The bust, besides being an admirable likeness, was an exquisite work of art, and it was gratifying to know that the cost of it was defrayed by a collection, almost entirely in pence, from the operatives.

Chapter IV

M R. PHILIP GRANT, in his "History of
Factory Legislation," says: "The sacrifice made by Lord Ashley can only be appreciated by those who best understood the
pecuniary position of this noble-minded man.
He had, at that time, a large and increasing
family, with an income not equal to many of
our merchants' and bankers' servants, and a
position as the future representative of an an-
cient and aristocratic family to maintain. Political power, patronage, social ties, family
comforts were laid down at the feet of the factory children, and freely given up to the sacred
cause of which he had become the leader."

Added to this was personal hostility and
fierce opposition from the Prime Minister, the
ruling statesmen, and the leading newspapers.
That all of this was hard to be borne appears
in his journal:

"By chance I picked up the *Morning Post*,

and found there the most violent and venom-
ous article I ever read against any public man,
directed against myself. This is only a sample
of the things which I endure. ' Were I just
coming into public life, I should die outright;
but though affected, I am acclimated, and
having endured other attacks, shall recover a
part of my health, but no more."

"The tone now is, among my adversaries,
'a well-meaning, amiable sort of man, with no
fragment of penetration.' "

"The *Times* charges me with weakness.
How can I be otherwise, not having in the
House even a bulrush to rest upon? 'No poli-
tician!' 'No statesman!' I never aspired to
that character; if I did I would not be such a
fool as to attack every interest and one-half of
mankind, and only on behalf of classes whose
united influences would not obtain for me fifty
votes."

He had, however, a firm friend in Prince
Albert and Queen Victoria. The Prince had
said when the position was offered Lord Ash-

ley which he declined to accept: "I have asked
that a peer be appointed to my household;
but if I can get such a man as Lord Ashley, I
will gladly take a man from the House of
Commons."

In his journal he speaks often of the
Queen's interest in him and his work:

"I am here at Windsor Castle by desire of
Her Majesty. From the hour she became
Queen to the present day, I and mine have received one invariable succession of friendly
and hospitable acts."

"Dined last night at the palace. I can not
but love the Queen; she is so kind and good
to me and mine. Poor soul! she was low-
spirited. O that she knew what alone makes
a yoke easy and a burden light!"

On one occasion Prince Albert said to him:
"We want to show our interest in the working classes, and we have sent for you to advise
us how to do it."

Lord Ashley had an answer ready: "Put
yourself at the head of all social movements

which bear upon the poor. On the 18th of May next, the anniversary of the Laborer's Friend Society will be held, and if your Royal Highness will accompany me, first to see some of the dwellings of the poor, and afterward to preside at the meeting, I am satisfied it will have a good effect."

The Prince at once fell in with the suggestion. But when some of the lords heard thereof, they were frantic with fear, and brought to bear every possible objection. Lord Ashley encouraged the Prince to persevere in his intention, as he finally did. With his brilliant cortège he visited house after house in Lord Ashley's company, and was everywhere received with great enthusiasm. Later, when he took the chair at the meeting, he "made it the occasion for the speech which first fairly showed to the country what he was."

The little touches of domestic life and affection, as they appear in Lord Ashley's records, are very tender and beautiful. Beginning with

the first anniversary of his marriage-day, he
says: "Mark this day with the red letters of
joy, hope, and gratitude. How much more I
should enjoy this visit to Oxford if Minny
were with me! I can not bear the shortest
separation from her." He says concerning
the christening of his little son:

"May God, in his mercy, grant that as the
child was this day signed with the sign of the
Cross, so he may never be ashamed to confess
and fight for a crucified Savior!"

"Took a walk with Minny. Much interesting conversation with the darling. She is a
most bountiful answer to my prayers. Often
do I recollect the very words of my entreaties
to God, that he would give me a wife for my
comfort, improvement, and safety. He has
granted me to the full *all* that I desired, and
far *more* than I deserved. Praised be his holy
name!"

"Minny is gone, and I am all alone—not a
bairn with me. I now taste by separation
more truly the blessings of God's goodness.

His gracious bounty has þestowed upon me a wife and children—and such a wife and such children!"

"My four blessed boys brought me to-day some money for the bishopric at Jerusalem. They offered it most willingly, even joyfully."

"Minny and I, through God's mercy, took the sacrament together. Afterwards, towards evening, we had a walk on the seashore, while the blessed children ran about the sands. We recalled the past, and anticipated the future in faith and fear and fervent prayer."

Lord Ashley next turned his attention to the "climbing boys" employed by chimney sweeps. For more than a hundred years the miseries of these poor little creatures had been kept before the public by philanthropic individuals, and yet their wrongs were not abolished. Little children from four to eight years of age, the majority of them orphans, inveigled from poorhouses, or apprenticed by poor-law guardians, or sold by brutal parents, were trained to force their way up the long, narrow,

winding passages of chimneys to clear away
the soot. In order to do this, they had to
move up and down by pressing every joint in
their bodies against the hard and often broken
surface of the chimneys; and to prevent their
hands and knees from bleeding, the children
were rubbed with brine. Their skin being
choked with soot, they were liable to a frightful disease called chimney-sweeper's cancer,
involving one of the most terrible forms of
physical suffering. They began the day's
work at four, three, or even two in the morning. They were half stifled by the hot sul-
phurous air in the flues, and often they would
get stuck in a chimney, and become unconscious from exhaustion and foul air. They
lived in low, ill-drained, ill-ventilated cellars,
and often slept on the soot-heaps. They remained unwashed, and on Sundays they were
generally shut up together, so that the neigh-
bors might not see their miserable condition.
They were morally and intellectually degraded
to the lowest possible point. Out of three

hundred and eighty-four boys examined by
the Commission, only six could write and
twenty-six could read very imperfectly. The
labors of Lord Ashley in Parliament were, as
a rule, the least part of his work on behalf of
any cause he espoused; and it was so in this
case. He went to see the climbing boys at
their work; he confronted the masters; he
took legal proceedings at his own expense as
"test cases," and even made provision for life
for the poor little sufferers whom he was able
to rescue from their living death.

In his speech he said that he had no idea
that cruelties so barbarous could be practiced
in any civilized country as had come under his
notice. It was a fact within his own personal
knowledge that a child four and a half years
old was at the present moment employed in
sweeping chimneys. The practice led not only
to loathsome disease, but also to extensive
demoralization. The children were sent up
without clothing, and often spent the night on
the soot-heap unclothed. As regarded the

demoralizing effect, he stated that there were
at that time twenty-three climbing boys in
Newgate for various offenses.

He became interested in a sweep whom he
first saw back of his own house in London.
He tried to buy him from his master; but the
master saw his advantage, and refused to re-
lease him. Lord Ashley sought the unnatural
father, and tempted his help by the offer of a
free education. This availed, and the boy,
who proved to be of a very lovable disposition,
was removed from his hateful bondage to a
boys' Christian school of a most pleasant sort.

The bill introduced by Lord Ashley, forbidding the employment by chimney-sweepers
of climbing boys, was opposed by the Duke of
Wellington, the great insurance companies,
and many of the lords who feared that the
safety of the metropolis was threatened.

He kept on pleading for the "four thousand
children who were at that time engaged in this
disgusting and unnecessary employment." At
last he took up the case of two little boys who

were suffocated in chimneys, and succeeded in having one of the masters arrested and sentenced to six months hard labor. Then the *Times* took up his cause, and in the agitation his bill was passed. His records have this item, which every reformer should read: "Let no one ever despair of a good cause for want of helpers. Let him persevere, *persevere*, PERSEVERE, and God will raise him up friends and assistants!"

We are convinced that Lord Ashley must have been an orator of no small power. A "word-portrait," written in 1838, says:

"Lord Ashley possesses the purest, palest, stateliest exterior of any man you will see in a month's perambulation of Westminster; indeed, it would be difficult to imagine a more complete beau-ideal of aristocracy. His delivery is fluent; his voice rich and fine in tone. When he addresses an audience he stands with his hand resting on the platform rail; he looks his hearers directly in the face, and with a very slight bowing movement, barely sufficient to

save him from the appearance of stiffness, he
delivers, without a moment's hesitation, and
with great dignity of voice and manner, a
short, serious address. The applause with
which he is always heard seems rather an in-
terruption than a pleasure to him. I have
heard that his lordship is very nervous, and
yet his most striking feature is self-possession,
which he never loses for a moment."

His biographer said of him near the close
of his life:

"Of the thousands of speeches made by
Lord Shaftesbury on every conceivable subject, he was always guided in their preparation
by a few simple rules. He did not write his
speeches, and never used notes. He got together all his evidence and everything he
wished to quote, and these he put in shape;
but the connecting matter he never formally
prepared. He thought the subject well over,
made himself master of the facts, and trusted
for the rest to the inspiration of the moment.

It was a saying of his, that it was not of great consequence how a speech was commenced, but it was all-important how it ended, and he almost always prepared his peroration, sometimes committing it to memory."

Chapter V

WHILE still a student, Lord Ashley became greatly interested in the study of Hebrew, declaring that he loved and venerated the Jews and everything that concerned them. We find him sending money to a Hebrew convert in Jerusalem, saying that he wished to revive the practice of apostolic times, and "make a certain contribution for the poor saints that are at Jerusalem!"

He prevailed on Parliament to ask for protection and encouragement for the Jews, and through his instrumentality a vice-consul was appointed from the nation and a bishop from the Church, who were to establish an Anglican bishopric in Jerusalem, and build a church on Mount Zion. He said in his plea:

"For centuries, the Greek, the Romanist, the Armenian, and the Turk have had their places of worship in the city of Jerusalem.

The pure doctrines of the Reformation have
alone been unrepresented amidst all these cor-
ruptions."

Frederick William IV, King of Prussia, who
had always been interested in the Jews, proposed that the two nations unite in the support of the bishopric, and so include all Protestant Churches in the Holy Land within its
pale. This brought forth hearty "Te Deums"
from Lord Ashley, who felt that the desire of
his heart was being realized. He wrote: "The
beginning is made, please God, for the resto-
ration of Israel. Our bishops can not endure
the notion of a *Jew* elevated to the episcopate.
They remember that Moses says, 'They shall
be a byword,' and forget that Paul declares
them 'beloved for the Father's sake.' The
order of Providence now seems to be, that in
proportion as we have abased the Jew, so shall
we be compelled to abase ourselves. His future dignity shall be commensurate with his
past degradation. Be it so; I can rejoice in

Zion for a capital, in Jerusalem for a Church, and in a Hebrew for a king."

Lord Ashley never had a shadow of doubt that the Jews were to return to their own land, that the Scriptures were to be literally fulfilled, and that the time was at hand. Indeed, it was his daily hope and prayer. He always wore on his right hand a ring, on which was engraved, "O pray for the peace of Jerusalem!" The words were engraven on his heart as well.

In 1843, Lord Ashley took up official alliance with a cause which, for more than forty years, was to receive his advocacy. He spoke against the opium trade with China, which was the first great indictment of the opium trade ever uttered within the walls of Parliament.

The history of the exportation of opium to China by the East India Company is briefly this: The company began enriching itself by the cultivation of opium, and the sale of it to Dutch merchants and others. Then the opium was clandestinely sold to the Chinese. Some of the East India officials and London directors objected to the importation of opium into China against the wishes of its rulers. But they pocketed the revenue, and openly sold the drug in Calcutta to merchants who shipped it off to China. Chinese authorities issued edicts enforcing severe penalties on the importation. But the company compensated merchants who had suffered loss through Chinese interference. The intelligent class in China saw that the nation was becoming enfeebled by the growing use of opium. The emperor determined on a bold stroke. He had his commissioner seize and destroy twenty thousand chests of smuggled opium. England declared war, and defeated the Chinese in spite of their gallant resistance, and by the Treaty of Nankin five ports were thrown open to the British trade, twenty-one million dollars were paid by China as a war indemnity and as compensation for the destroyed opium, and Hong Kong became a British possession.

But in spite of all pressure brought to bear on them, the Chinese steadily refused to legalize the opium-traffic, although it was useless to try to enforce laws against it.

Such was the state of affairs when Lord Ashley began his long crusade against the opium trade. The first words on the subject in his journal are about the war:

"I rejoice that this cruel and debasing opium war is terminated; but I can not rejoice (it may be unpatriotic) in our successes. We have triumphed in one of the most lawless, unnecessary, and unfair struggles in the records of history; it was a war on which good men could not invoke the favor of Heaven, and Christians have shed more heathen blood in two years, than the heathen have shed of Christian blood in two centuries!"

When he was preparing his speech he wrote:

"O what a question is this opium affair! Bad as I thought it, I find it a thousand times worse, more black, more cruel, more Satanic

than all the deeds of private sin in the records
of prison history. O God, be thou with me
in the hour of trial, and touch my lips, like
Isaiah's, with fire off the altar!"

He brought the subject before the House
of Commons by moving, "That it is the opinion of this House that the continuance of the
trade in opium, and the monopoly of its
growth in the territories of British India, are
destructive of all relations of amity between
England and China, injurious to the manufacturing interests of the country by the very
serious diminution of legitimate commerce,
and utterly inconsistent with the honor and
duties of a Christian kingdom; and that steps
be taken as soon as possible to abolish the
evil."

He declared that he had no hostile feeling
toward the East India Company, that they
had conferred great benefits on the Empire
they were appointed to govern, and the guilt
was not theirs exclusively; it was shared by
the Legislature and the whole nation.

5

From the testimony of witnesses, he
showed that all Chinese society, from the im-
perial family down to the lowest ranks, suffered from the baneful effects of the drug, that
officials were corrupted and multitudes ruined,
and that the trade was a source of danger,
shame, and disgrace to all concerned. He
showed that no progress had been made in
commerce with China; testimony was overwhelming that the Chinese were anxious for
trade, but the opium-traffic stopped the way.
He then proceeded to give a vivid description
of the general effects upon its victims, of in-
dulgence in opium as a luxury; their physical,
mental, and moral debility; their hideous dis-
figurement and premature decay, resulting in
misery almost beyond belief, destroying myriads of individuals annually, and casting its
victims into a bondage with which no slavery
on earth could compare, and from which there
was scarcely a known instance of escape. It
stood in the way of the progress of society,
the civilization of man, and the advancement

of the gospel. Opium and the Bible could not
enter China together. He showed them that
the Baptist Missionary Society had decided to
work through the agency of American missions, because the public feeling in China was
so strong against the English, that if the missionaries hoped to work at all, it must be
through America, which had kept aloof in a
great degree from the disgraceful traffic. So
it had come to this, that England, which professed to be at the head of Christian nations,
was shut out by her own immoral conduct
from sending her own missionaries to that
part of the world which she herself had opened
for civilization and Christianity!

He demanded that Parliament should destroy the monopoly which the East India
Company possessed, of the growth and manufacture of opium in India, and prohibit the
cultivation of the drug in the territories of the
East India Company.

The Prime Minister, Sir Robert Peel, asked
him to withdraw his motion. He indulged in

a line of argument, the gist of which was that as we could not put down gin at home, we need not concern ourselves about introducing twenty thousand chests of opium into China every year.

The *Times* said that Lord Ashley's speech was grave, temperate, and practical, well stored with facts, authorities, and arguments, and more statesmanlike in its views than those by which it was opposed, whose arguments amounted to this:

"That morality and religion, and the happiness of mankind and friendly relations with China, and new markets for British manufactures were all very fine things in their way; but that the opium trade was worth £1,200,000 a year; and upon the whole we could not afford to buy morality and religion, and the happiness of mankind and friendly relations with China, quite so dear."

His journal has this entry:

"Last night, opium! Though I did not succeed in carrying my motion, yet I made a sensible impression on the House, and, I hope, on the country. I was, perhaps, more master of myself than on any former occasion, yet down to the very moment of commencing my speech I was in great dejection. God was with me, and I reached the consciences, though I could not command the support of several members. Spoke for nearly three hours; nevertheless, the House listened to me throughout with patience and sympathy."

In 1840, Lord Ashley moved in the House that a humble address be presented to Her Majesty to direct an inquiry to be made into the employment of the children of the poorer classes in mines and collieries, and in the various branches of trade and manufacture in which numbers of children work together. He said in conclusion:

"I have been bold enough to undertake this task because I regard the objects of it as beings created as ourselves, by the same Maker, redeemed by the same Savior, and destined to the same immortality. It is in this spirit I entreat the investigation and removal of those sad evils which press so deeply and extensively on such a large and such an interesting portion of the human race."

After a short discussion, the motion was agreed to, and a commission granted,—a convincing proof of Lord Ashley's power as a social reformer in the House of Commons.

In 1842 the report of the commission was issued. A mass of misery and depravity was unveiled, of which even the warmest friends of the laboring classes had but a faint conception.

A very large proportion of the workers underground were less than thirteen years of age; some of them began to toil in the pits when only four or five. Young, timid children descended the steep shafts into mines which were always damp, dark, and close; water trickled down the sides; the floor was ankle-deep in black mud, and all around a labyrinth of dark, gruesome passages.

The first employment of a very young child

was that of a "trapper." The ventilation of a
mine was a complicated affair not easily explained. Suffice it to say, that were a door or
trap left open after the passage of a coal-carriage through it the consequences would be
very serious, causing perhaps an explosion.
Behind each door, therefore, a little child or
trapper was seated, whose duty it was, on hearing the approach of a whirley or coal-carriage,
to pull open the door, and shut it as soon as
the whirley had passed. From the time the
first coal was brought forward in the morning,
until the last whirley had passed at night—
that is to say, for twelve or fourteen hours a
day—the trapper was at his monotonous work.
He had to sit alone in the pitchy darkness and
the horrible silence, unable to stir for more
than a dozen paces with safety, lest he should
be found neglecting his duty and suffer accordingly. He dared not go to sleep—the
punishment was the "strap," applied with
brutal severity. The mines were infested with
rats, so bold that they had been known to run

off with the lighted candles in their mouth, and explode the gas. All the circumstances of a little trapper's life were full of horror, and upon nervous, sensitive children the effect was terrible, producing a state of imbecility and ofttimes idiocy. Except on Sunday, they never saw the sun; their meals were eaten in the dark, and they had no hours of relaxation.

As they grew older, the trappers were passed on to other employments, "hurrying," "filling," "riddling," "tipping," and occasionally "getting," and in these labors no distinction whatever was made between boys and girls in their mode of work, in the weights they carried, in the distances they traveled, or in their dress, which consisted of no other garment than a ragged shirt or a pair of tattered trousers. "Hurrying"—that is, loading small wagons with coals, and pushing them along a passage—was a barbarous labor, performed by women as well as by children. They had to crawl on hands and knees, and draw enormous weights along shafts as narrow and as wet as common sewers. When the passages were very narrow, and not more than eighteen or twenty-four inches in height, boys and girls performed the work by girdle and chain; a girdle was put around the naked waist, to which a chain from the carriage was hooked and passed between the legs, and, crawling on hands and knees, they drew the carriages after them. Their little bodies were bruised and blistered from contact with the walls, and their ankles strained out of all human semblance. They did the work of beasts of burden, because human flesh and blood was cheaper in some cases, and horse-labor was impossible in others.

"Coal-bearing"—carrying on their backs on unrailed roads burdens from half a hundred weight to one hundred weight and a half—was almost always performed by girls and women, and it was a common occurrence for little children of six or seven years to carry burdens of coal of half a hundred weight up steps that, in the aggregate, equaled an ascent fourteen times a day to the summit of St. Paul's Cathedral! The coal was carried in a basket formed to the back, the straps of which were placed over the forehead, and the body had to be bent almost double to prevent the coals from falling. Sometimes these straps would break in ascending the ladder, when the consequences would be serious to those who were following.

Another form of severe labor to which children as young as eight years of age were frequently put, was that of pumping water in the under-bottom of the pits. The little workers stood ankle deep in water, performing their unceasing tasks during hours as long as those in the other departments of labor, and were sometimes required to work thirty-six hours continuously. In addition to the hard labor, the apprenticed children suffered terribly from the cruelty of the overlookers, who bargained for them and used them as they pleased. Brutal punishments were inflicted for trifling offenses, and the food of the children was al-

ways insufficient and of the coarsest sort. Of
course, these little beasts of burden suffered
terribly in health, and lived short lives. Acci-
dents of falling down the shaft, coal falling
upon them, suffocation by gas, drowning from
the sudden breaking in of water, were of the
most common occurrence, which better regulations and machinery have now made very
rare.

Education was totally neglected, and the
morals of the people were in the lowest possible state. Wages were unreasonably low,
and in some districts they were paid in goods
from a neighborhood shop, where the neces-
saries of life were very much dearer than else-
where.

For all the revolting cruelties practiced
upon the poor children in mines and collieries;
for all the dreadful sufferings to which they
were subjected; for all the horrible indecencies
daily passing before their eyes; for all the ignorance, licentious habits, and social disorgan-
ization springing out of this state of things,

the main excuse given was, that without the employment of child-labor the pits could not possibly be worked with a profit; that after a certain age the vertebræ of the back do not conform to the required conditions, and therefore the children must begin early. Furthermore, unless early inured to the work and its terrors, no child would ever make a good collier.

Lord Ashley exposed the iniquity of the system in a speech so powerful, that it not only thrilled the House, but sent a shudder through the length and breadth of the land.

For two hours the House listened so attentively that even a sigh could be heard, broken only by loud and enthusiastic applause. Many men wept, and a dozen members spoke in quick succession praising Lord Ashley, and pledging themselves to his holy cause. Mr. Richard Cobden, a man of very great influence who had opposed Lord Ashley every step publicly and privately, raised no objection whatever to the Mines and Collieries Bill. On

the contrary, when Lord Ashley had concluded his great speech—a speech he always
considered one of the most successful he ever
delivered—Cobden came over to him, wrung
his hand heartily, and said: "You know how
opposed I have been to your views; but I
do n't think I have ever been put into such a
frame of mind in the whole course of my life
as I have been by your speech." He subsequently declared that from that hour he was
perfectly convinced of the genuine philanthropy of the noble lord.

Prince Albert wrote him:

"MY DEAR LORD ASHLEY,—I have carefully perused your speech, and I have been
highly gratified by your efforts, as well as
horror-stricken by the statements which you
have brought before the country. I know you
do not ask for praise, and I therefore withhold
it; but God's best blessing will rest with you,
and support you in your arduous but glorious
task. I have no doubt but that the whole

country must be with you—at all events, I can assure you that the Queen is, whom your statements have filled with the deepest sympathy. It would give me much pleasure to converse with you on the subject. Believe me, with my best wishes for your total success,

"Ever yours truly,   ALBERT."

The Mines and Collieries Bill, introduced by Lord Ashley, asked that all women and children be excluded from coal-pits. It is quite impossible to understand the prolonged trouble and anxiety Lord Ashley had to encounter in putting his bills through Parliament. It was always easier to move the House of Commons than the House of Lords. In this case we find him saying:

"Much, very much trouble to find a peer who would take charge of the bill. It is 'the admiration of everybody, but the choice of none.' So often refused that I felt quite humbled. Disappointment and apprehension lie heavy on me. I sent the bill to the Lords with

deep and fervent prayer, committing it to
God, as Hannah consigned her son Samuel to
his blessed service. May he, in his mercy,
have respect unto me and my offering! Were
it not for public opinion, I should not be able
to carry *one particle* of the bill. The promises
of the ministry are worth nothing."

The long period of anxiety and disappointment came to an end at last. The bill, which
was one of the greatest boons ever granted to
the working classes, passed the House of
Lords successfully. The victory is recorded
thus:

"Took the sacrament on Sunday in joyful
and humble thankfulness to Almighty God for
the success with which he has blessed my effort for the glory of his name and the welfare
of his creatures."

Chapter VI

THE poor were constantly in Lord Ashley's thoughts. If he was weary with incessant labors, he would say: "I am reminded of the poor seamstresses and factory women. How tired they must get!"

If he was ill, he would compare his luxuries and tender care with the sufferings of the sick who could not afford medical attention, nor even the barest comforts of life. His biographer says:

"He was never too proud to grasp the hand of a poor honest man, or take up a sickly little child in his arms, or sit in the loathsome home of a poor, starving needlewoman as she plied her needle. He never spoke down to their level, but sought to raise them up to his, and his kindly words were as helpful as his kindly deeds."

On one occasion, when addressing an assembly of young men, he said:

"Depend upon it, the time will come when you will bless God if your career has been one by which your fellows have been benefited and God has been honored. Christianity is not a state of opinion and speculation. Christianity is essentially practical, and I will maintain this, that practical Christianity is the greatest curer of corrupt speculative Christianity."

How truly he practiced his own theory we may know from every page of his life.

When in 1848 there was an outbreak of cholera in London, and every one who could was running out of the city, Lord Ashley, with his colleagues on the Board of Health, was working night and day in the very midst of the plague. Reviled by the newspapers, hampered by red-tape, he persevered in his labors; and be it remembered that it was entirely unpaid service which he rendered throughout the whole of the difficult and dangerous time of the existence of the Board of

6

Health. He cared not that his service was unappreciated, but he wanted his physicians to be known. He said: "I am unable to speak with adequate praise of the medical staff, miserably paid as they are. They have labored even to sickness, and when struck down by the disease have hastened back to their work, not for emolument (for they received fixed salaries), but for conscience' sake. And such are the men whose scanty recompense certain gentry would reduce by ten per cent."

Lord Ashley was troubled because in this perilous time there was no turning to prayer. In vain he appealed to the bishop and archbishop. Not until there was a panic caused by two thousand deaths in one week, was there a call for special prayer in the churches. But not until the terrible summer had passed, and a fairly clean bill of health could be returned, did Lord Ashley allow himself the rest which he so sorely needed.

Night after night he tramped off to East London to meet his various societies of poor

people, or to lead an evangelistic service. His
journal has this record:

"It seems occasionally a wearisome journey
to undertake on dark and rainy nights; but
I always rejoice when there—all is earnest,
pious, simple, and consolatory. The care-
worn faces of the men and women become almost radiant with comfort."

On the grand occasion of the army encamp-
ing on his estate, Lord Ashley set forth in his
little open carriage to meet the general and
his staff. On the road he met an old woman
hobbling along; he at once stopped, gave her
his place in the carriage, and himself mounted
the box! In this way he drove up to the spot
where, in the presence of the Prince of Wales
and dukes, he was to be received with all military honors as lord-lieutenant of the county.
And he was absolutely unconscious that there
was anything singular in the manner of his
arrival!

In 1851, Lord Ashley's father died, and he
became the Earl of Shaftesbury. He wrote

on the day of his father's funeral: "And now I bear a new name which I did not covet; and enter on a new career, which may God guide and sanctify! If I can by his grace make the new name attain but to the fringes of his honor and the welfare of mankind, I shall indeed be thankful."

Some time before the death of his father, Lord Ashley had determined not to take his seat in the House of Lords. But to use his own expression, "The leading of Providence was the other way." His two Lodging-house Bills would soon pass the Commons, and he **must himself pilot them through the House of Lords.**

It is needless to say that there was genuine sorrow that "Lord Ashley" had left the House of Commons. Sir Robert Inglis made it the occasion to speak of him on this wise:

"During the last fifteen years of Lord Ashley's Parliamentary life he has been emphatically the friend of the friendless. Every form

of human suffering he has, in his place in this
House, sought to lighten; and out of this
House his exertions have been such as, at
first sight, might have seemed incompatible
with his duties here. But he found time for
all, and when absent from his place on these
benches he was enjoying no luxurious ease,
but was seated in the chair of a Ragged School
meeting, a Scripture-reader's Association, or
a Young Men's Christian Institution. I will
add no more than that the life of Lord Ashley
in and out of this House has been consecrated,
in the memorable inscription of the great
Haller, 'To Christ as found in the person of
the poor!'"

In June, 1851, Lord Shaftesbury (as he will
hereafter be known) took his seat in the House
of Lords, and on the evening of that day he
wrote in his journal:

"It seems no place for me; a 'statue gal-
lery,' some say a 'dormitory.' Full half a
dozen Peers said to me within as many min-

utes, 'You 'll find this very different from the House of Commons: no sympathies here to be stirred.' "

The following day he made his first speech in the House of Lords. It was in behalf of the inspection and registration of lodging-houses. He spoke in a low tone of voice and with great brevity, and took occasion to explain that it was the deep interest he felt in the objects of this bill, and the urgency there was for legislation on the subject, "that had induced him to address their lordships so early after his call to their lordships' House."

It was an unprecedented occurrence for one member to carry a measure through all its stages in both the House of Commons and the House of Lords. This was, however, accomplished by Lord Shaftesbury, and his bill became law. It has been acted upon throughout the kingdom, and police authorities, magistrates, medical men, city missionaries, and all whom it concerned, have been unanimous in their testimony as to its beneficial results.

Charles Dickens said to Lord Shaftesbury
some years afterward, "That is the best law
that was ever passed by an English Parliament."

Let us look for a little at the breadth of
Lord Shaftesbury's sympathies and service.
In 1850, Mrs. Harriet Beecher Stowe wrote
"Uncle Tom's Cabin." For years Lord
Shaftesbury had watched every movement
bearing upon American slavery. He had been
distressed beyond measure by the Fugitive
Slave Law, by which "a whole nation, blessed
by God with freedom, wealth, and the Holy
Scriptures, declares it to be impossible to
emanicpate a slave, and penal to teach any one
of them the first principles of Christianity."

He wrote to Mrs. Stowe to express his
admiration of her work, and his gratitude to
God, who had stimulated her heart to write it.
He then drew up an address from the women
of England to the women of America, asking
them to consider how far the system of slavery
was in accordance with the Word of God, the

inalienable rights of immortal souls, and the
pure and merciful spirit of the Christian religion. In course of time the "Address" went
forth, signed by tens of thousands of the women of England.

While Lord Shaftesbury was engaged in
this anti-slavery agitation, many of the American papers attacked him with great severity,
and urged him to turn his attention to the
working classes of his own country. The ed-
itor of one of the religious papers of the South
was greatly roused, and in an angry article he
wrote:

"And who is this Earl of Shaftesbury?
Some unknown lordling; one of your modern
philanthropists suddenly started up to take
part in a passing agitation. It is a pity he does
not look at home. Where was he when Lord
Ashley was so nobly fighting for the Factory
Bill and pleading the cause of the English
slave? We never even heard the name of this
Lord Shaftesbury *then*."

Lord Shaftesbury enjoyed a good joke, and he often told this story with great relish.

Be it known that this nobleman, Lord Shaftesbury, was called the "Father" of the Shoeblack Brigade. The Brigade was organized just before the great Hyde Park Exhibition of 1851. It was Lord Shaftesbury who established regular stations, and "set up" these friendless, penniless little fellows in a business which brought them one thousand pairs of shoes a day to be cleaned, and an income of twenty-five hundred dollars. To-day the Brigade is one of the permanent institutions of the land, having educational extensions and social improvements of many kinds.

In 1855 the army of the Crimea had a terrible winter. The *Times* declared that "The noblest army England ever sent from these shores has been sacrificed to the grossest mismanagement. Incompetency, lethargy, aristocratic hauteur, official indifference and stupidity, reign, revel, and riot in the camp before

Sebastopol, in the harbor of Balaklava, and in the hospitals of Scutari."

"Every day fresh tidings came of privation, sickness, and death; of unspeakable suffering from neglect; of medical stores decaying at Varna that were intended for Scutari; of tents standing in pools of water for want of implements to dig trenches; of consignments of boots all for the left foot; and so forth. One good came out of the evil, destined to affect every battlefield for all future time; namely, the landing in Scutari of Miss Florence Nightingale and the noble band of women who accompanied her as nurses to the sick and wounded. Thus was inaugurated the Geneva Red Cross Association, which has since done so much to mitigate the horrors of war."

In the face of fierce opposition in the War Department and from political lords, Lord Shaftesbury bent all his energies towards the organization of a Sanitary Commission to proceed with full powers to Scutari and Balaklava, there to purify the hospitals, ventilate the ships, and exert all that science could do to save life where thousands were dying, not of their wounds, but the result of bad sanitary conditions. Florence Nightingale wrote Lord Shaftesbury some time afterwards, "That Commission saved the British army!"

In the city of Florence there dwelt two small shopkeepers, Francesco and Rosa Madiai. They were simple, sincere, common people, who, under the influence of Protestant teaching, were led to regard the Church of Rome as in error. The Scriptures became their delight, and although warned not to read them, they persevered, and endured patiently the persecution which followed. The matter was then referred to the Grand Duke of Tuscany, who condemned them to five years' imprisonment with hard labor in the galleys. When this story reached the ears of Shaftesbury, he wrote Prince Albert, calling his attention to it. The King of Prussia was asked to make a joint representation with the Queen, and send a deputation to intercede with the

Grand Duke. The deputation set forth, but was unable to effect anything. The Grand Duke replied:

"They are Tuscan subjects, and have been condemned to five years' of punishment for propagating Protestantism, which is forbidden by our laws as an attack upon the religion of the State."

Lord Shaftesbury at once announced that he would start off in search of the Madiai. He agitated the subject before Parliament and in the newspapers. All the country was aroused, and the Grand Duke could no longer stand the storm of indignation which he had aroused. The Madiai were set at liberty.

We would expect that Lord Shaftesbury would take a lively interest in the Sepoy Rebellion, as he did. He had the courage to arraign the Government of India. He urged repeatedly that, instead of "harping upon that odious word, *neutrality* in religion, there should be a distinct and manful acknowledgment of Christianity on the part of the Gov-

ernment." Throughout this anxious period,
when the past and future of English dominion
in India were in question, he showed them
that the revolt had opened up a wide and noble
field for Christian enterprise, and he urged
upon all missionary societies the necessity of
sending forth missionaries and copies of the
Bible.

When peace was restored, he began an investigation of the factory system of India,
which resulted in an Address to Her Majesty,
praying her to instruct the Viceroy of India to
take into immediate consideration the necessity of passing a law for regulating the labor
of women and children in the factories of India. The movement was a success as far as
Lord Shaftesbury was concerned. The bill
was passed in India, but has not accomplished
all that was designed, because there was no
public opinion in India to demand that its
provisions be enforced.

The high position Lord Shaftesbury maintained in the political world, and his reputation

as a lover of humanity, made him to be sought
by men of all nationalities. Thus it happened
naturally that those who were struggling for
the freedom of Italy wrote Lord Shaftesbury.
He replied with a letter of fervent sympathy
and commendation. This brought a letter
from Garibaldi, as follows:

"MY LORD,—You have, in two letters published in the papers, done justice to the Ital-
ians, and have assumed the patronage of their
noble cause. I express to you, in the name of
my country, the deepest sense of gratitude.
Accept, my Lord, that of a soldier and your
devoted   G. GARIBALDI."

Lord Shaftesbury replied, urging Garibaldi
to come in person and receive a manifestation
of hearty approbation. He declared that the
great general, "as the representative of a generous and oppressed people struggling for civil
and religious liberty, would call forth such an

expression of national feeling as would be, if possible, equal to the occasion and the merits of the man."

In 1864, Garibaldi came to England. Lord Shaftesbury was his constant companion the whole of the time he was in London, never leaving him, in fact, except when Garibaldi "*would* go to the opera."

One of the subjects which particularly interested Garibaldi during his visit was Lord Shaftesbury's work in relation to the housing of the poor. He obtained all the information he could, with a view to the construction of better dwelling-houses for the working classes in Italy. When they parted, Lord Shaftesbury presented him with a copy of the New Testament in Italian. It had this interest attached to it, that it was the only copy of the Scriptures that was finished printing while Garibaldi was in Rome. In giving it, Lord Shaftesbury begged him, as a personal favor, that he would read it, and this Garibaldi prom-

ised he would do. He left in Lord Shaftesbury's hand a little note full of tender thankfulness.

"Of that name," said Lord Shaftesbury,
referring to Garibaldi in a speech, "no man can
speak without emotion. He is a man that rep-
resents in himself the best qualities that adorn
mankind."

In 1863 all civilized nations were thrilled
with horror at the cruel manner in which Russia was engaged in putting down an insurrec-
tion in Poland. The tyranny of Russia had
provoked some bloody struggles, and when
in 1861 some thirty thousand Poles were assembled near a battle-field engaged in singing
hymns and prayer for the souls of those who
had fallen, and the Russian cavalry rushed in
and slaughtered numbers of them, intense national feeling was kindled. The indignant
populace joined in other demonstrations of a
patriotic character, and the result was fresh
massacres by the Russian soldiery. The Poles
were forbidden to meet together, even in the

churches, and all who were mourning for rela-
tives killed in the massacres were severely pun-
ished. The great nations tried to intervene
diplomatically, but their remonstrances were
utterly disregarded by the Czar. "Everywhere in Poland blood was flowing freely, and
the midnight sky was red with the flames of
burning villages and homesteads. Fines and
confiscations brought all the wealthier inhab-
itants to the verge of ruin, and the whole population of suspected villages was put to the
sword."

A great meeting convened in the name of
the Lord Mayor in London, to express English sympathy with the Poles. Lord Shaftesbury made the address, which he considered
the greatest speech he ever made. Referring
to it twenty years afterward, he said, "It tore
me to pieces to deliver it." When he was
pleading the cause of oppressed nationalities
his utterances had a peculiar pathos and
power. It was in vain that the great nations
used all of their diplomacy and moral influ-

ence. Poles were executed, driven off to Siberia in crowds, and Poland lost her last item of independence.

The Franco-Prussian war brought him an immense increase of labor and anxiety. He set forth the Christian duty of relieving the horrors of war. He urged that the distribution of help be given equally to French and Germans. The result of his agitation was the establishment of the National Society for Aiding the Sick and Wounded in time of War," of which Lord Shaftesbury became president, and in whose operations he took an active part.

Thus the loving thought and care of this great-hearted man included equally the little friendless child and the nations of the earth.

Chapter VII

L ORD SHAFTESBURY'S interest in the
religious life of England is no small part
of his own history. In 1836, when he was
only thirty-five years of age, he presided at
a meeting of clergy and laity to discuss the
best method of "extending the means of
grace in and to necessitous parishes, in strict
conformity with the spirit, constitution, and
discipline of the Established Church."

The result of this meeting was the establishment of the Church Pastoral Aid Society
—"for the purpose of benefiting the population of our own country, by increasing the
number of working clergymen in the Church
of England, and encouraging the appointment of pious and discreet laymen as helpers
to the clergy in duties not ministerial."

The Society at once met with opposition
and condemnation. It was declared that it

99

was started without Episcopal sanction, and was false to the principles of the Church. The High Church party objected to the lay agency to be employed. Some contended that the laymen should be only those who were candidates for holy orders. Many bishops, who were willing that laymen should labor for the spiritual welfare of those around them, objected to a distinct order of lay teachers, who, they claimed, would not be amenable to ecclesiastical authority.

The Society was desirous to be at peace with all men, and yet it was unwilling to abandon lay agency. It finally compromised by declaring that lay agents might be employed in destitute places, even if not candidates for holy orders, but they would be under the direction of the clergy of that district. When this decision was announced, Gladstone (then a young man of twenty-six), who had been vice-president of the Society, withdrew, and established an institution called "The Additional Curates' Society."

Shaftesbury's biographer writes: "The first years of the existence of the Pastoral Aid Society were years of trial, difficulty, and ceaseless controversy, and entailed upon Lord Shaftesbury an enormous amount of labor. His good judgment, his tact in smoothing down differences, his experience of the requirements of poor and neglected parishes, his patient attention to the details of every new move of the Society, and the influence of his tongue and pen, were invaluable at this time. For nearly fifty years he was hardly ever absent from the chair on the occasion of the annual meeting, and always reserved for that meeting the full expression of his opinion on the state of the Church and the signs of the times. His speeches on behalf of the Pastoral Aid Society give the religious history of nearly half a century.

"Lord Shaftesbury was appalled to find, from reliable authority, the state of spiritual destitution prevalent in many parts of the country. He was surprised to learn from offi-

cial documents that one hundred thousand
souls were, in spite of every effort, annually
added to those who, in Protestant England
and under the wing of an Established Church,
had neither pastors, sacraments, nor public
worship, but were left unheeded, with no man
to care for their souls. It was this sense of
ever-increasing need that urged him to make
the Pastoral Aid Society the efficient institution it has become; and from first to last he
claimed for it, in spite of all argument to the
contrary, full recognition as a Church of England Society, regarding the wants of the
Church on the one hand, and observing the
order of the Church on the other."

In 1841 and 1842 there was a crisis in the
history of religious thought in England. Ra-
tionalism, imported from Germany, was making rapid advances; but the Church was in far
greater danger from "foes within." The High
Church party issued "Tracts for the Times,"
as they were called, being, indeed, statements
favorable to popery and the confessional. The

University of Oxford was the center of the
Tractarian movement, but every section of the
Christian Church felt its influence. The principal leaders of the Oxford School were the
"seraphic Keble," Richard Froude, Dr. Pusey,
and John Henry Newman. Their claim was
that the real Catholic Church was the Church
of England; that the successors of the apostles
were to be found in her. "The battle of the
Reformation had to be fought over again,"
and for forty years Lord Shaftesbury was one
of the leaders in the fight on the Evangelical
side. He wrote to Sir Robert Peel, who was
about to become Prime Minister:

"The Church will present more serious difficulties than any other matter of Government.
There are now within its bosom two parties,
divided against each other on principles irrec-
oncilable, heart-stirring, and vital. The party
denominated the Puseyites are strong in number, possess character and learning, but are
confined chiefly to the clergy. Their opponents are the majority, but do not enjoy the

advantage of being concentrated in a university; they have more piety and less reading, but carry with them the great body of the laity. These parties regard each other with the greatest dislike and suspicion. The Puseyites consider their opponents as little better than Dissenters, the Evangelicals look upon the Puseyites as almost papists. The Puseyites assert that the Evangelicals depreciate the authority of the Church and the Fathers; the Evangelicals maintain that the Puseyites prefer it to the Bible. My purpose is to point out to you the consequences that must come from the elevation to high ecclesiastical offices of persons distinguished for the new opinions. The Church will be shaken by violent commotions. My belief is that many of that party are actually Romanists in creed, and will declare themselves to be such, whenever conscience gets the better of Jesuitry." This last was a prophecy which was fulfilled in due time.

The Puseyites put forward as candidate for the chair of Poetry at Oxford a man who pro-

mulgated their views. Lord Shaftesbury refused to vote for him, and instead supported a
man with Evangelical sympathies. Shaftesbury's man was elected. His correspondence
with his opponents, Dr. Pusey (who was his
cousin) and Rev. John Keble, show the spirit
in which he conducted his opposition. He
writes to Dr. Pusey:

"Every one, however deep his piety, however holy his belief, however simple and perfect his reliance on the merits of his Redeemer,
is consigned by you, if he be not episcopally
ruled, to the outer darkness of the children of
the devil, while in the same breath you desig-
nate the Church of Rome as the sweet spouse
of Christ, and hide all her abominable idol-
atries under the mantle of her bishops. This
is, to my mind, absolutely dreadful.

"For yourself, I must ever entertain real
kindness and esteem. No one, amidst all this
conflict of passion and principle, has at any
time doubted your sincerity and devotion. It
is sad that we differ, but let not that difference

amount to enmity. I have enough of foes; my public course has begotten me many haters among the powerful and wealthy. You and I have now lived more than half our time, according to the language of the psalmist. We are hastening to the grand end of all things, and then may God lead you unto living fountains of water, and in his mercy wipe away all tears from your eyes!"

Closing a letter to Keble, he writes:

"Perhaps you have forgotten, what I well recollect, that you were one of the examining masters when I took my degree some nineteen years ago. Your amiable and gentleman-like demeanor then made an impression on my mind which has never been effaced. I can not take leave of you without adding that I shall always think of you with respect, not unmingled with affection."

In 1844, Keble wrote: "We go on working in the dark, and in the dark it will be, until the rule of systematic confession is revived in our Church."

An effort was then made to get an endowment for a Catholic college, which was successful.

The next move was by the Church of Rome, declaring that England had been restored to the Romish communion, and would henceforth be ecclesiastically governed by the **new hierarchy.**

A great meeting was held in London to invoke aid for the suppression of Romish innovation in the Church of England. Lord Shaftesbury presided, and in a great speech full of wise forecasting and burning patriotism he made a profound impression, which produced immediate results. The Roman Catholics in England saw with regret the results of their policy. They sent up an address of loyalty to the Queen, and asserted the purely spiritual character of their organization. A Roman Catholic peer publicly regretted the ill-advised measure of the Roman pontiff, which had placed English Catholics in the position of having "either to break with

Rome, or violate their allegiance to the Queen." The more prominent Puseyites went over to the Catholic Church, and Lord Shaftesbury thanked God, and took courage.

Who but a leader of great wisdom and mighty influence could have led the multitudes through those trying times?

Lord Shaftesbury, although a Protestant of the Protestants, entertained most charitable views towards Catholics. He voted and worked for Catholic emancipation. He was a trusted co-worker with a big-hearted Catholic woman, who was carrying out a colonization scheme. He always spoke with deepest respect of the Sisters of Mercy, who went about doing good. It was only when clergymen of the Established Church, whose hearts were with the pope, sought to get control of the Church, or to seize or enslave his country, that he assumed a bold defensive.

As we shall see, he found the Established Church cold and apathetic and very conservative concerning the philanthropic reforms which were of such vital interest to him. When he was trying to get the Ten-hour Bill for factory women, he wrote: "I find, as usual, the clergy are in many cases frigid; in some few, hostile. At first I could get *none*. I fear that many of them are timid, time-serving, and worshipers of wealth and power. I can scarcely remember an instance in which a clergyman has been found to maintain the cause of laborers in the face of pewholders."

On another like occasion he wrote plaintively: "As usual the 'saints' were against me, and the 'sinners' were my helpers."

His journal has this record:

"To-day I presided at a Mothers' Meeting in Westminster. A wonderful, a miraculous spectacle! It was a sight to bless God for; such a mighty reformation of drunken, idle, profligate, dirty, and cruel parents! As usual, none of the clergy were there. A work of this kind, and of this high and spiritual character, effected by an unordained person, a humble layman, who, without the intervention of a bishop or a college education, had nothing but the grace of God and the Holy Scriptures, is too powerful, too convincing, too irresistible. It overwhelms 'apostolical succession' by an avalanche of practical truth."

His creed was of the simplest sort. This is revealed in a record made one Good Friday:

"As I taught my little children to-day, it seemed to me wonderful in how small a compass is contained the whole sum and substance of Christian religion. Volumes without end, years of study, years of controversy, immense thought, immense eloquence, all expended, and mostly wasted, to dilate or torture that which may be comprehended by the understanding and relished by the soul of a simple child. What will all the learning of the world add to the plain facts of the fall of man and his salvation by Jesus Christ?"

He said to his biographer:

"I am an Evangelical of the Evangelicals. I have worked with them constantly, and I am satisfied that most of the great philanthropic

movements of the century have sprung from
them. I believe in the necessity of a 'new
birth' through the revelation to each individual soul, by the agency of the Holy Spirit and
the Word. I believe in the Christian life as a
humble, continuous trust in the Atoning
Blood, a simple faith in Scripture, a constant
prayerfulness, and a recognition of the hand
of God in all the events of life.

"I believe that the sole remedy for the dis-
tracted state of the Church is to do what we
can to evangelize the people by preaching on
every occasion and in every place, in the
grandest cathedral and at the corner of the
street, in the royal palace and in the back
slums, preaching Christ to the people. I do
believe that the preaching of Christ is still the
power of God unto salvation. If it has ceased
to produce its effect, it is because so many of
the sermons (not from Church of England
pulpits alone, but also from some Nonconformists), instead of setting forth the gospel
in its simple yet majestic power, are mere milk-

and-water dilutions of the saving truths. This may satisfy fine folks, but the great mass of the poorer sort of people and our agricultural laborers will either have religion of the best quality, or none at all. I have been very much among this class, and I know that the religion for them is that which addresses itself to their inmost affections, softens all their sorrows, and alleviates their miseries by showing them that they have the sympathy of their fellow-men and the still higher sympathy of a Heavenly Father.

"I remember one night at the George Yard Ragged School. A magic-lantern had been purchased to interest the poor things, and I went down to have a talk with them. Some pictures on the Life of Christ were to be exhibited. There were about four hundred people in the room, and the police told me that between four and five hundred were turned away. The interest in the pictures was intense, and I shall never forget their earnest, excited faces as the scenes in the sacred drama passed before them. The last picture represented our Lord standing beside a closed door, and the text at the foot of the picture was, 'Behold, I stand at the door and knock.' The effect was startling; it seemed to bring the story home to every heart, and when I said, 'What you see there is going on at the door of every house in Whitechapel,' they were moved to tears. It was a revelation to them, and when I told them that if they would throw open the door He would 'come and sup with them,' there was something so cozy and comfortable to them in the idea of it, that they came pouring round me and thanking me. Poor, dear souls! they do not care much for churches and chapels and the outward forms; they like their religion to be cozy. It fills them with hope of what may some day be their lot, for now they have no comforts in their lives. I wonder how it is they do not die of despair!"

As late as 1855 Lord Shaftesbury found an unrepealed law forbidding gospel teaching and worship in private houses where, beside

8

the family, more than twenty persons were gathered. Any religious gathering not under the protection of the Established Church might be dispersed. Lord Shaftesbury moved for its repeal. He presented the facts: millions of non-church-goers; all the Churches together unable to overcome the prevailing immorality and infidelity; and this law in full force, which could shut up every Sunday-school, Cottage School, Ragged School, and city mission. Strangely enough, he encountered fierce opposition. Some said that the decree was a dead letter. He replied that "a dormant reptile is not dead, and may be warmed into life when occasion serves."

Lord Shaftesbury, with his accustomed zeal, investigated the working of the law, and found that it had been repeatedly used for purposes of intimidation, and he quoted a case in which it had been enforced:

A gentleman, a county magistrate in a northern county, early in 1854, came to reside on his estate, and found the parish in a most

neglected condition. At the gates of his park
was a large coal-mine, and a dense population
around it. One evening in every week he
went to the largest cottage, read a chapter of
the Bible and some religious tracts. The
meetings were largely attended; but after a
few months he was obliged to close the service. And why? It was hinted to him that persons were about to bring information against
him for a breach of the Conventicle Act. He,
being an active county magistrate, felt that it
was not right in him to set an example of
breaking the law, so he gave up his reading.
The gentleman might have had a cock-fight
or any sort of amusement, and nobody would
have objected to it, but the moment this gentleman, commiserating the religious destitution of the people, went to their cottages, read
to them a chapter in the Bible, and joined with
them in religious worship, the law said, "Mind
what you are doing, for if you are caught at
this again, you will be fined £20."

Eleven bishops opposed the repeal of this

law, and finally offered a clause granting permission to offer prayer in opening or closing a service. The very idea of "permission" to pray was intolerable to Lord Shaftesbury.

"It may as well be said," he exclaimed, indignantly, "that I am to have permission to breathe the air!"

The law was repealed by a majority of one vote.

In speaking of the opposition which met him in his own Church, he said:

"They call me a Dissenter and the greatest schismatic who was ever produced. A schismatic, according to the Bible, is one who denies the doctrines which Christ taught. But to apply this word to one because he can not conform to all the decrees of the bishops and every form of priestly assumption is, I hold, a great profanation of the word, and a want of principle in the man who so dares to use it."

He was so in the habit of looking at every question from the standpoint of the poor, that when the subject of Evening Communion was being considered by the clergy, he made a strong plea in favor thereof. He said:

"We must remember that vast numbers of these people have not a moment's leisure from domestic duties until the evening, and the rectors of large parishes tell me that for one poor man or woman who has attended morning communion, fifteen have attended evening communion. And it is the testimony of those who have witnessed such scenes, that it is quite refreshing to observe the earnest, humble, and devout manner in which these poor creatures assemble around the table of their blessed Lord. If it is announced that the ministers do not care to consider their convenience and necessities, they will certainly stay away from the churches altogether. And how, I ask you, in such a refusal, can the Church of England call herself the 'Church of the People?'"

He was a warm advocate of open-air preaching, and, in fact, was an open-air

preacher himself, having spoken most effect-
ively on such occasions.   He said of them:

"I look upon these services as perfectly
normal; they are certainly primitive.   The
very earliest preaching of the gospel was in
the open air, on the shores of the Lake of Gali-
lee, by our blessed Lord himself.   And they
are unquestionably ecclesiastical.   In the earliest times of the Reformation there was open-
air preaching at Paul's cross.   All the wor-
thiest of the bishops preached there; there,
too, Bishop Latimer preached to hundreds
those words of truth which brought forth
good fruit."

In 1857 we find Lord Shaftesbury rejoic-
ing that a special religious service was to be
held in Exeter Hall on Sunday evenings.
They were designed to bring the clergy and
people more closely together, and to remove
the impression that the clergy were "only gentlemen who wore black coats and received
large salaries."   They appealed especially to
the working classes, by providing that there

should be no distinction of persons, no reserved seats, no collections, and, in short, that
every one should be on the same footing as if
he were the first man in the land.

Twelve services were held, and, notwithstanding the heat of the weather, five thousand
eager listeners thronged the hall, and half as
many more were sent away for want of room.

At this juncture the clergy of that parish
forbade the minister who had been engaged
to officiate at those unusual services. Although Lord Shaftesbury doubted the legality
of the inhibition, his judgment was overruled,
and the services were stopped. Application
was made for another hall, but this clergyman
was afraid of an irregular service, and forbade
it. Just here the Nonconformists came to his
help, and of them he declared in his speech:

"To the members of the Nonconformist
body we owe a debt of gratitude for the manner in which our places have been supplied.
They have, in this instance, acted with a deli-
cacy and a forbearance which redound infi-

nitely to their credit. They declined to engage
Exeter Hall until they had ascertained that it
would be quite impossible for us to renew our
services; and having taken the hall, they offered to give it up whenever we might desire.
They selected the hymns which we used to
have sung, and the officiating minister read a
lesson and a portion of the Litany of the
Church of England, while in his discourse he
never, directly or indirectly, alluded to the
difficulties under which the Church of England was placed, or to the freedom of the party
to which he belonged."

Lord Shaftesbury proposed a clause to the
Religious Worship Act which would legalize
these services, but it was refused. The Archbishop of Canterbury introduced a bill making necessary the sanction of the bishops, and
this was carried, and after some delay the
sanction was obtained.

In 1860 seven great theaters were opened
for religious worship, with an average attendance of twenty thousand people. Lord

Shaftesbury often led those vast meetings himself. It was an interesting sight when he stood upon the stage, Bible in hand, and read a chapter of the "sweet story of old." From floor to ceiling, the great house was thronged: costermongers, street-cadgers, and laborers; women in fluttering rags, many with babies in their arms; boys in their shirt-sleeves; young men and maidens in their gaudy "Sunday best." Before the service there was much confusion, but when the opening prayer was offered, the silence throughout the whole house was intense and solemn. When Lord Shaftesbury rose to read the Scripture, there was a buzz of approbation. Like the priests in Ezra, he "read in the book of the law of God distinctly, and gave the sense, and caused them to understand the reading," and thereby touched their hearts and consciences. When the preacher told the simple story of the gospel of Christ, the people listened as if they had never heard the subject before.

It soon became apparent that these services

were accomplishing a vast amount of good. As we might expect, the movement did not meet with universal approval. A certain Lord Dungannon arose in the House of Lords "to call attention to the performance of divine service at the theaters Sunday evenings, and to move a resolution that such services were highly irregular, and calculated to injure the progress of sound religious principles."

Lord Shaftesbury, "the only culprit in the House, and one of the principal movers in originating these services," replied. IIis speech was the most interesting of its kind ever heard in that august House. With terrible earnestness, in graphic language, he held his audience for nearly three hours as he told the story of the movement. He quoted letters from the chief of police, testifying that at every service the people had conducted themselves with the greatest propriety. In conclusion, he said:

"My lords, you must perceive the rising struggle to get the gospel. Will you say to

these destitute and hungering men, 'Come, if
you like, to Episcopal Churches, and there you
shall be preached to in stiff, steady, buckram
style? We will have you within walls consecrated in official form; otherwise you shall
never hear from us one word of gospel truth!'

"Do you admit that the Church of England
is bound so tightly by rule and rubric? In
that case the people will reply: 'Let the Nonconformists do the work then, but let the
Church of England take up her real position
as the Church of a sect, and not that of a nation!'"

It was perceived that Lord Shaftesbury had
the sympathy of a majority of the House, and
Lord Dungannon withdrew his motion.

Contrary to what one would expect, Lord
Shaftesbury was not in sympathy with the Salvation Army movement. When it was only
a year old, he was invited to join. He refused,
and gave his reasons. He felt that the ex-
cesses of the Army produced great irreverence
of thought and action, turning religion into

a play, and making it grotesque. He could not believe that the proceedings were founded on Scripture.

He acknowledged that there was need of an increase of lay missions in the great city, and he spoke with great respect of the gifts and influence of General and Mrs. Booth, while he commended their temperance work as the strongest point of the Salvation Army.

Lord Shaftesbury was a stout opponent of the revision of the Bible. But after the revision appeared, he acknowledged that his fears had not been realized. He feared that the sturdy Saxon would be set aside for Frenchified or Italian words. He speaks lovingly of the "racy old language, which is music to everybody's ears, and which, like Handel's music, carries divine truth and comfort to the soul." He rejoiced to know that the King James Version was not set aside, but loved and studied more than before.

For the Young Men's Christian Association Lord Shaftesbury entertained an almost

parental affection, and was wont to speak of
its members as his sons. He said: "I have always looked upon this association and all kin-
dred associations in all parts of the United
Kingdom and in America as grand cities of
refuge."

In 1875, Moody and Sankey commenced a
series of "revival-meetings" at Islington.
Lord Shaftesbury contributed to the fund, and
regarded the arrival of Mr. Moody as that of
the right man at the right hour. His description of the service is most interesting as coming from a Church of England man. He says:

"The music was the simplest possible,
adapted to the poorest and least taught mind.
And yet it went to the inmost soul, and
seemed to empty it of everything but the
thought of the good, tender, and lowly Shepherd. The preacher was clad in ordinary
dress; his language was colloquial, abounding
in effective illustrations, often bordering on
the humorous. The voice was ill-managed.
There is no eloquence, and yet the result is

striking and effective. These two simple, unlettered men from the other side of the Atlan-
tic have had no theological training and never
read the Fathers; they are totally without skill
in delivery, and have no pretensions to the
highest order of rhetoric. God has chosen
the foolish things of the world to confound the
wise. Moody will do more in an hour than
Canon Liddon in a century. I agree with
Gamaliel, 'If this thing be of men, it will soon
come to naught; but if it be of God, ye can
not fight against it.' To my mind there is
something in it superhuman."

Lord Shaftesbury's friendship with Mr.
Spurgeon, the well-known Baptist minister of
the Metropolitan Tabernacle, was close and
beautiful. In spite of the eccentricities of his
early days, Lord Shaftesbury prophesied that
his great gifts would become the inheritance
of the whole Church of Christ.

Chapter VIII

I N 1843, Lord Shaftesbury first turned his
attention toward the Ragged School question. For some years the condition of the
waifs, the vagrants, and outcasts of London
had been a source of great anxiety ·to him.
Because they seemed utterly neglected and
left to perish, soul and body, his big loving
heart took them in. But the problem of how
to reach them and how to hold them was a
great one. It was in his thought day and
night. And in the meantime he saw that
there was growing up in London an enormous
population of thieves and vagabonds. He did
not know of any effort that was being made
to reclaim them. "They lived in filthy dwellings or under arches; they begged or stole;
they grew up in horrible ignorance of everything that was good, and with a horrible
knowledge of everything that was evil; and

sooner or later they became acquainted with the prison or the hangman."

One February day, Lord Shaftesbury read in the *Times* this advertisement:

RAGGED SCHOOLS.

FIELD LANE SABBATH-SCHOOL

"The Teachers are desirous of laying before the public a few facts connected with this school, situated in this most wretched and demoralized locality. It was opened in 1841 for instructing, free of expense, those who, from their poverty or ragged condition, are prevented from attending any other place of religious instruction. The school is superintended by the London City Mission, and is opened on Sunday and Thursday evening with an attendance of seventy adults and children. The teachers are encouraged by the measure of success which has attended them. But money and teachers are needed at once to give permanency to a work of charity, commenced and supported by a few laymen whose means are inadequate."

Lord Shaftesbury said: "I never read an advertisement with keener pleasure. I could not regard it as other than a direct answer to my frequent prayer."

The first reply to this notice was from him. He entered heartily into the movement, and from that day to the close of his life he was the champion and leader of every effort in behalf of Ragged Schools.

He made himself personally acquainted with every detail of the work, and the neighborhood in which it was carried on. Field Lane, where the Ragged School was situated, was one of the most disreputable parts of London. It was in the heart of what was known as "Jack Ketch's Warren," so named because a great number of the people who were hanged at Newgate came from this district. The disturbances which occurred here were of so desperate a character that policemen visited it in companies of forty or fifty, well-

9

armed men, it being unsafe to act in fewer numbers.

"For a century this district had been the resort of the most notorious evil-doers. Some of the houses were close beside the Fleet Ditch, and were filled with dark closets, trap-doors, sliding panels, and other means of con-cealment and escape, while extensive base-ments served for the purpose of concealing stolen goods, and in others there were furnaces used by coiners. On the north side of the street were a number of tenements fearful to approach, called Black Boy Alley. The method pursued by the Black Boy Alley Gang was to entice the unwary by means of prosti-tutes: then gag them so that they could not give the alarm; after which they would drag their victims to one of their dens, and, hav-ing robbed and murdered them, throw their dead bodies down into the ditch. These atrocities became so common that special steps were taken by the Government to pursue

the offenders, nineteen of whom were executed at one time."

In such a locality as this the Ragged School
work was born. It was not long before Lord
Shaftesbury was as familiar with this district
of Field Lane as with the neighborhood of
Grosvenor Square, where he lived. Only a
genuine love for human beings could have
drawn Lord Shaftesbury from his happy home
to these loathsome haunts, where visitors must
close their senses to sickening sights and
sounds and smells.

Charles Dickens described his visit to this
Ragged School when it was first started, and
again after Lord Shaftesbury had taken it
under his protection.

"I found the Ragged School pitifully struggling for life under every disadvantage. It
had no means; it had no suitable rooms; it
derived no power or protection from being
recognized by any authority; it attracted
within its walls a fluctuating swarm of faces,

young in years, but youthful in nothing else. It was held in a low-roofed den, in a sickening atmosphere, in the midst of taint and dirt and pestilence, with all the deadly sins let loose, howling and shrieking at the doors. The teachers knew little of their office. The pupils derided them, sang, fought, danced, robbed each other, seemed possessed by legions of devils. Some two years ago I found it quiet and orderly, lighted with gas, well white-washed, numerously attended, and thoroughly established."

Under Lord Shaftesbury's direction there was established a free day-school for infants; an evening school for youths and adults; a woman's evening school to teach housekeeping and other domestic arts; industrial classes to teach youths tailoring and shoemaking; a home for boys; a night refuge for the utterly destitute; a clothing society for the naked; a distribution of bread to the starving; baths for the filthy; Bible-classes, through which about ten thousand persons were brought to know the gospel story; a school missionary, who scoured the streets and brought in the wanderers; and a Ragged Church for the worship of God.

"Having taken the matter in hand, he at once proceeded to get a firm grip of it by seeing for himself everything that was to be seen in connection with the work, and hearing for himself all that was to be heard. He went into the vilest rookeries, and became acquainted with the most ignorant and depraved. He visited the few Ragged Schools that were in existence at that time, and inspired hope and courage in the teachers by his presence. He took his place in the school beside them, and spoke kindly words to the wondering listeners.

A strange sight was a Ragged School audience in those days. There were to be seen the cunning expression of the cadger; the sharp, acute face of the street minstrel; the costermonger out of work; the cropped head of the felon, who had just left prison; the pallid and thinly-clad woman weakened by long-continued sickness and penury; the spare form of him who, once in affluence, had wasted his substance in riotous living. And among this motley assembly Lord Shaftesbury would sit, with his calm eyes gazing sorrowfully upon them, and his pleasant voice trying to utter words of hope."

When he saw what was being accomplished in one district, he longed to have the work extend. Isolated efforts could not affect the general condition of the waifs and strays of the metropolis. There were thousands of the children of the lowest and most ignorant classes springing up, sturdy of growth as weeds in a wheatfield. "They swarmed the streets; they gamboled in the gutters; they haunted the markets in search of castaway food; they made playgrounds of the open spaces; they lurked under porches of public buildings in hot and wet weather; and they crept into stables or under arches for their night's lodging. They lived as the street dogs lived, and were treated much in the same way;

everybody exclaimed against the nuisance, but nobody felt it to be his business to interfere. The first practical effort to reach these street Arabs was to lure them to the Ragged Schools."

It was at just this time that three Ragged School teachers, men in humble positions, met and discussed the hardest problem of the day. They resolved, "That to give permanence, regularity, and vigor to existing schools, and to promote the formation of new ones throughout the metropolis, it is advisable to call a meeting of superintendents, teachers, and others interested in these schools for this purpose."

This was the beginning of the Ragged School Union. Lord Shaftesbury was very scrupulous about giving honor to whom honor was due, and when he was called the founder of the Ragged Schools he modestly declared that while he would rejoice if it were true, he was neither the founder of the schools nor the Ragged School Union.

This, however, is true, that from the time he joined the movement, it grew marvelously in importance and power, and for forty years his love and zeal in its behalf knew no abatement.

The Executive Committee consisted of Shaftesbury, William Locke, and Joseph Gent, whose names appeared in all public announcements and on the certificates of deserving scholars. Curiously enough, these names stood in a similar position two hundred and fifty years ago in a bit of history connected with America.

King Charles II gave to the first Earl of Shaftesbury a tract of land in America in the latitude of Charleston City. The two rivers bounding the city north and south were named Cooper River and Ashley River, in honor of the Earl. He framed a constitution for the embryo colonies, and called to his help the illustrious Locke and a man named Gent, who visited America, and whose emigrants built

the village which subsequently became the city
of Charleston.

Shaftesbury's biographer compares the
work of the two sets of men, and says: "The
labors of the latter trio have been to reclaim
the moral wilderness, to purify and cultivate
the moral wastes, and to set up spiritual fort-
resses that shall be unassailable by the great
enemy."

Public meetings were held in most of the
churches and halls of London and the large
towns. Lord Shaftesbury presided at these
occasions, and in short, earnest addresses set
forth the claims of the poor. He also was in
the chair at the quarterly-meetings, where
practical subjects were discussed and progress
was reported.

"For many years the ragged children of
London were rarely out of his thoughts, wak-
ing or sleeping. He visited them in their
wretched homes and at their daily work. He
sat beside them in their schools. He let them

come to his house to tell him their troubles. He pleaded for them in religious and political assemblies. He carried their cause into the House of Commons and into the House of Lords. He interested the whole country in their welfare, and, as we shall see, he achieved great things for them."

In 1846 he chose two companions, and explored the unknown parts of London to see for himself the alleys and lanes and houses in which the poorest of the poor and the lowest of the low dwelt.

One of his companions was a physician, and the other was a missionary.

Such a mission needed no ordinary man, and Lord Shaftesbury brought to it no ordinary gifts. He could enter an abode of filth and wretchedness where every sense was sickened, and appear perfectly at ease. He could win the confidence of the poor and outcast. He could benefit without patronizing, and preserve his own dignity amid the rough and lawless, without placing any barrier to mutual approach.

This great-souled man saw in the miserable creatures before him, "not thieves and vagabonds and reprobates, but men with immortal souls that might be saved, and with human lives that might be redeemed from their corruption. In the woman with unkempt hair and tattered garments, he saw, not the abandoned harlot, but the woman that was a sinner, who might yet be brought to the feet of Him who would say to her in the tenderest of human accents, 'Go, and sin no more.' "

His special sympathy went out to little children. He was throughout his life the champion and friend of children.

He was wont to say that the greatest compliment ever paid to him came from a little child. He was standing at a street crossing in the heart of London. A little girl stood at the curb, afraid to attempt going alone. She glanced from face to face with an anxious look, and then slipping her tiny hand into Lord Shaftesbury's and looking up into his face with a trustful smile, said, "Will you please carry me over?"

His biographer says: "It is no exaggeration to say that in the whole course of his life he hardly ever passed a ragged child in the street without the desire to stop and talk to it. Morning, noon, and night the welfare of the uncared-for and unthought-of children weighed upon his heart, and he looked upon any day as lost in which he did not do something to make the weariness of their lives less weary, and their sadness less sad. The words of the Master were ever ringing in his ears, 'Feed my lambs.'

"He possessed in perfection the art of speaking to children, and few men ever spoke to them with greater effect: not because he was a 'lord,' but because he could lay hold of the heart of a child, and because the whole bearing of the man impressed the fact that he was intensely in earnest. Year after year he had seen the law of kindness produce the most wonderful effects on the minds of the wildest, the rawest, the most ungovernable children. It was always through the children that he hoped to win the parents.

"Wherever he went, the people clustered about him in groups, and received him with respect."

In fact, throughout his life, although he went freely among vagrants, thieves, and criminals of every kind, he never received an insult. The people everywhere seemed grateful for his interest, and freely answered his questions.

He found a condition of things a hundredfold worse than he had thought possible. He found large populations packed into the area of a good-sized barn, without drainage, ventilation, or sunlight, where contagion and disease ran riot. He found that there were few house-rents so high as those paid by the veriest outcasts of the street.

"The tenant of a mansion paid a lower

nightly rent, in proportion to the space he occupied and the cubic feet of air he breathed,
than did the miserable urchin, who spent his
two or three pence for permission to stow himself under a bed of a low lodging-house filled
to suffocation by the most abandoned of all
ages—one of the twenty or thirty inmates of
a space not large enough for the accommo-
dation of more than two or three."

He made these facts public before an influ-
ential audience met with the "Society for Improving the Condition of the Working
Classes." He told his audience of rooms so
foul, that when a physician who was used to
such places visited them, he was obliged to
write his prescription outside the door. He
gave them graphic descriptions of courts and
alleys thronged with a dense, immoral population, defiled by perpetual habits of intoxica-
tion, and living amid riot and blasphemy, tu-
mult and indecency.

Lord Shaftesbury recommended that the
society erect a model lodging-house, where

human beings might have the decencies and comforts of life at a moderate rent. This was the beginning of the great model lodging-house system, which has transformed many of those London courts and alleys which were reeking with filth and misery into abodes of comfort.

His journal shows how the subject of Ragged Schools was absorbing him:

"April 28th.—This is my birthday. Although the day was very tempting here at home, I took the chair at a Ragged School as a sort of thankful offering and appropriate duty."

"May 29th.—Dined yesterday with ——. The courtesies of life and friendship demanded it. A splendid display of luxury and grandeur. The contrast was so great to the places where I have spent so many hours lately, that I felt almost uneasy. The few pounds, too, that I want, and shall not get, for the establishment of Ragged Schools, seemed wasted in every dish. A greater simplicity would be more

beneficial to the poor, to society, and to themselves. O, if some Dives would give me two
or three hundred pounds, the price of a picture or a horse, I could set up schools to educate six hundred wretched children!"

"June 12th.—I am now begging for four
objects. Busy in founding a Ragged School.
Alas! alas! I can set up a school, which shall
give education every evening to two hundred
and eighty children, for fifty-eight pounds a
year, hardly more than it costs to prosecute
one criminal—and yet I can barely collect the
sum!"

"July 6th.—Much rain yesterday. My
poor little children of the One Tan Ragged
School had a day in the country, and must
have been sadly disappointed because they
could not roll on the wet grass. Poor little
things! No doubt they bore it well—better
than we higher folks should have done.

"Do you want to read the story of a sturdy
beggar? Rambling in the lowest parts of
Westminster, I found a Ragged School held

in a deserted stable, cold and vile. I went
back to the House of Commons, stood at the
entrance of the House, and asked every one
whom I thought well disposed to the cause,
to give me a sovereign. Having got twenty-
eight pounds, I went back and ordered the
place to be put in repair. I was very proud
of the act then, and I am proud of it now."

In seven years after its organization, a hundred new schools were added to the Union,
attended by more than ten thousand children.
Lord Shaftesbury's labors multiplied with the
schools. Each had its opening ceremonies, or
its anniversary, or its prize distribution night.
It required constant diligence to perform the
duties devolving upon him. Conferences with
teachers, interviews, correspondence day after
day; and in all parts of London the inevitable
speeches night after night. Every detail of
the Union was in his thought and care. When
he saw that, as order was established and decent rooms were supplied, there was a tend-
ency to admit children of a class and con-

10

dition for whom the schools were not intended, he said:

: "So long as the mire and the gutter exist, you must keep the schools adapted to their wants, their feelings, their tastes, and their level. I feel that my business lies in the gutter, and I have not the least intention to get out of it."

He inspired the teachers with his own indomitable activity and courage. In a fervid address to them he gave utterance to this conviction:

"I tell you, my friends, that if, with all the success you have attained, with all the knowledge you have acquired, with all the blessings you have received, you pause in your course any longer than is necessary to take breath, gather strength, survey your position, and thank God—why, then, I say, never again come into this hall, for, if you do, I will be the first to say to you, as Cromwell said to the House of Commons, 'Out upon you! begone; give place to honester men.'"

The industrial classes, refuges, and homes, which were the outgrowth of the Ragged School Union, all felt the touch of his sympathy and the wisdom of his guidance.

The workers met with a good many discouragements. The districts were flooded by a periodical deluge of the miserable population of Ireland. The best results of the work were removed by the emigration scheme which Lord Shaftesbury subsequently started. No support came from the Government, and but very little from the wealthy classes. And yet Lord Shaftesbury was able to say: "We have organized a system of prevention by which to stop crime while it is in the seed, and sin before it has broken into flower and desolated society. We maintain that every one of those whom we have reclaimed would, from the very necessity of his position, have been either a thief or a vagabond."

One feature of the Ragged School system was the gift of a prize to each scholar who had remained in one situation for twelve months

with satisfaction to his employer, and for good
conduct. Lord Shaftesbury always gave these
prizes, and his addresses to the children on
these occasions overflowed with "fatherliness"
and loving interest.

He never lost an opportunity of saying ad-
miring words for the Ragged School teachers.
He thrilled his audiences with stories of their
zeal and courage. He declared that he saw at
Field Lane school the most remarkable exhibition of human nature and the most beautiful
testimonial to woman's influence that he had
ever beheld in all his life:

"I have there seen men of forty years of
age and children of three in the same room—
men the wildest and most uncouth, whom it
was considered dangerous to meet, and perhaps it would be dangerous to meet them in
the dark alone; but in that room they were
perfectly safe. I saw there thirty or forty men,
none of them with shoes and stockings on, and
some without shirts—the wildest and most
awful-looking men you can imagine. They all

sat in a ring, and the only other human being
in the room was a young woman less than
thirty years of age, and, allow me to add, one
of the prettiest women I ever saw. She was
teaching all of those wild, uncouth creatures,
who never bowed the head to any constable
or any form of civil authority, yet they looked
on her with a degree of reverence and affection that amounted almost to adoration.
Meeting the superintendent, I said: 'My good
fellow, I do n't like this; there she is among
all those roughs. I am very much alarmed.'
'So am I,' he said. 'Then why do you leave
her there?' I asked. He replied: 'I am not
alarmed from the same reason that you are.
You are alarmed lest they should offer some
insult to her; but what I am afraid of is this,
that some day a man might drop in, who, not
knowing the habits of the place, might lift a
finger against her, and if he did so, he would
never leave the room alive; he would be torn
limb from limb.' So great was the reverence
that these lawless and apparently ungovern-

able creatures paid to the grace and modesty of that young woman."

In 1860 the Ragged School teachers made a presentation to Lord Shaftesbury of an oil-painting illustrative of the benefits of his work. It was accompanied by an elegantly bound volume, containing an address beautifully engrossed, to which was appended the signatures of no less than seventeen hundred subscribers. The signatures were of all sorts and conditions of men. In replying to the address, Lord Shaftesbury said:

"I would rather be president of the Ragged School Union than have the command of armies or wield the destiny of empires. That volume, with its valuable collection of signatures, will show to our posterity that some have been good enough to say that I have not been altogether useless in my generation."

The painting hung over the mantelpiece in the dining-room at Grosvenor Square; the volume was kept in a case in the room, and both were shown with pride and pleasure to visitors to the very close of his life.

Lord Shaftesbury took a strong personal interest in every individual for whose behalf he labored.

A letter written in 1849 was found, thirty-six years after its date and shortly after his death, in the box which he always carried about with him, as containing the things he most valued. It is written in a cramped, ill-formed hand, with some misspelled words, and is addressed: "Lord Ashley, Exeter Hall, Westminster, London." On the cover Lord Shaftesbury had written, "Very precious to me, this letter." It ran thus:

"PORT ADELAIDE, SOUTH AUSTRALIA.

"MOST NOBLE LORD,—I arrived at Port Adelaide after a pleasant passage, and am now in a comfortable situation and with very pious people. I have need to thank you for your kindness in sending me out. I think with per-

severance I shall do much better here than in
England. I do not think I shall ever forget
the good advice I received at Palace Yard
Ragged School, and sincerely thank them all
for their kindness.

"Please to accept the thanks of your obliged
and thankful servant,

"CAROLINE WALKER."

On the back of the letter, written evidently
many years later, is the following:

"She went into service, behaved so well
that her master gave her in marriage to his
son. She became a considerable person in
Australia, and afterwards went to India.
Where is she now? God be forever with this
Ragged School girl!   SHAFTESBURY."

A friend who called to see Lord Shaftesbury found him in his library at Grosvenor
Square, with two portraits before him. One
was that of a poor, puny, destitute child in rags
and tatters. The other was a handsome wo-

man in fashionable attire. He held them up before his guest: "Just look at these portraits. They have rejoiced my heart more than I can tell. I am more delighted than if I had become possessed of half the kingdom. Years ago, late at night, there was a knock at the door. Somehow it attracted my attention more than usual. Presently I heard the angry voice of a man in altercation with my servant. I felt a strange prompting that it was my duty to go and see what was the matter. There was a man with a little child in his arms, which he was endeavoring to thrust into the arms of my servant, who, of course, would not take it. 'What is all this about?' I asked. The man turned to me, and said: 'Lord Shaftesbury, I have brought this child to you. I do n't know what else to do with it. I can not trust myself to be its father, and I can not abandon it altogether.'

"I let the man in, and took down from him all particulars, and the end of it was that the child was left with me. I did not know very

well what to do with the poor little thing, so
I had her sent to an inn close by for the night,
and the next day when she was here, a lady
happened in who knew of a home where a
child was wanted. The mistress of the home
liked the child, and adopted her. And that
portrait of the fine lady is the portrait of what
that little ragged, destitute child has developed into. I feel as convinced that I was
moved to do what I did by our blessed Lord
as if I had seen him in person and heard his
voice."

Some one asked Lord Shaftesbury if he did
not find a good many hopeless cases. He was
aroused at once.

"Hopeless, indeed! Why, look at my
friend 'Punch'—as we called him. Punch had
been a source of annoyance to almost all the
workhouses of the metropolis. He showed.
himself to be one of the most abandoned
scamps in London. At last he came to the
Refuge in Great Queen Street. Seeing him
there, I said to him: 'Punch, how can you go

on in this way? You have got some good
about you; you have good abilities and you
have strength. Shall we make a man of you,
Punch?'

"Punch replied, 'Well, I do n't mind if
you do.'

"We set about trying, and, by God's blessing, we did make a man of him. Having been
made a first-rate shoemaker, he set out to
Natal to carry on business there, where I hope
he is maintaining the honorable character
which he had when he left the Refuge."

Many stories are told of Lord Shaftesbury's
love for homeless children.

A little girl who was sheltered in one of the
Refuges, which had a new dormitory to be furnished by subscriptions, took it upon herself
to write to him, and ask him for a subscription.
She had no name but Tiny:

"DEAR LORD SHAFTESBURY,—You will see
by the address that I have changed my home
from Albert Street, where I remember you

spoke to me, and told me about your dog. If
you please, Lord Shaftesbury, I want to ask
you if you will give a bed to our new home.
Fifty of the girls from the highest division
have been sent from Albert Street here, and
we have contributed the cost of one ourselves
out of our little store. You will come, I hope,
and see our new home. I am sure you will
like it, for I do, and my sister is with me.
Please come and see the pictures a gentleman
gave us. I remain yours respectfully,

"TINY."

This was his reply:

"MY DEAR SMALL TINY,—I must thank
you for your nice letter, and say that, God willing, I will certainly call and see your new
home, and you, too, little woman. You ask
me to give a bed to the new home. To be
sure I will. I will give two if you wish it, and
they shall be called 'Tiny's Petitions.'

"I am glad to see how well you write. And
I shall be more glad to hear from your friends

that you are a good girl, that you read your
Bible, say your prayers, and love the blessed
Lord Jesus Christ. May he ever be with you!
"Your affectionate friend,
                              "SHAFTESBURY."

In 1871 we find this record in his journal:
"I ran to Whitechapel to-day to see a little
piece of stranded seaweed—a poor, parentless
girl of eight years old, whom God, in his goodness, has manifestly intrusted to my care. I
sent her in emigration to Canada with a religious family. May the Lord bless her in
body and in soul!"

The Refuge and Reformatory Union,
which was an outgrowth of the Ragged
School movement, ultimately came to have
five hundred and eighty-nine homes, accom-
modating fifty thousand children!

Three hundred thousand children were
brought under the influence of the society!

To estimate the blessing which this single
movement brought to the neglected classes of

England by simply looking at the statistics, would be like calculating the blessing of sunlight by trying to weigh the sunbeams. In that army of lawless, ignorant street arabs was the embryo of an English Revolution, which in development would have turned the peaceful kingdom into a battlefield of terror and bloodshed.

Chapter IX

IN 1848 the spirit of revolution was abroad
in all Europe. Louis Philippe, King of
France, was expelled from his capital, his palace plundered, and himself cast down to a private station. Riots and turbulence were
everywhere. All Englishmen were driven out
of France with circumstances of great oppression and dishonor. They were not allowed to
bring away even their property, nor to receive
their arrears of wages. They were denied employment and public relief, and were met at
the savings bank where their earnings had
been deposited with the answer of "No funds."
They crowded the French outposts, and
begged to be sent back to their own country.

Lord Shaftesbury originated a scheme for
the relief of refugees, six thousand of whom
were brought over, cared for on their arrival,
and passed on to their respective destinations.

In England the Chartists were demanding their rights, and shouting, "Dissolve the Parliament!" "Give us the People's Charter!"

The great demonstration by the Chartists, for which the nation had prepared strong military defense, and concerning which it felt great alarm, proved to be not at all terrifying. The meeting at no time exceeded thirteen thousand people. We must believe that Lord Shaftesbury's sympathy and influence with the turbulent classes had not a little to do with the peaceful ending of what threatened to be a dangerous riot.

Although there was distress in the manufacturing districts, the people showed their appreciation of Lord Shaftesbury's kindness by remaining tranquil, some thousands of the operatives enrolling themselves as special constables.

When the panic was over, Sir George Grey, Home Secretary, wrote to him, and thanked him for his valuable aid.

The *Times* acknowledged that his influence

had been of a pacific sort in perilous times,
even though political economists and men of
the world did vote Lord Shaftesbury a bore.

The *Morning Chronicle* had an editorial of
this sort:

"No thinking man concurs with Lord
Shaftesbury; but it is a very good thing in
these days to have a nobleman who brings forward the distresses and needs of the people,
and gives them assurances that their case will
be considered."

The next great practical question which engaged Lord Shaftesbury was that of emigration. In the June of 1848 he brought forward
in the House of Commons this motion:

"That it is expedient that means be annually provided for the voluntary emigration to
some one of Her Majesty's colonies of a certain number of persons of both sexes, who
have been educated in the schools ordinarily
called Ragged Schools, in and about the metropolis."

The speech was a fine piece of oratory,

11

filled with vivid descriptions and interesting anecdotes, and with statistics, which in his speeches were never dry bones, but full of life and thrilling interest. He announced at the beginning that as he was not introducing a controversial question, or assailing any inter-est, he did not expect any opposition, except from those who believed they could suggest a better plan. He declared that he brought forward his plan, not from any overweening confidence that he had hit the only true method, but from a desire to excite discussion and stimulate thought in this direction. He stated that, through the London city mission-aries and Ragged School teachers, he had come to know of these thirty thousand naked, filthy, roaming, lawless, and deserted children, quite distinct from the ordinary poor. He said:

"Till very recently the few children that came under our notice in the streets and places of public traffic were considered to be chance vagrants or beggars, who by a little exercise

of magisterial authority might be either extin-
guished or reformed.   It has only of late been
discovered that they constitute a numerous
class, having habits, pursuits, feelings, cus-
toms, and interests of their own; living as a
class in the same resorts, perpetuating and
multiplying their filthy numbers."

He described to the House the habits and
dispositions of this wild race, their pursuits,
manner of life, and dwelling-places.   He examined sixteen hundred of these Arabs, and
found that nearly two hundred had been in
prison many times.   A hundred of them had
left the places they called home because of ill-
treatment.   One hundred and seventy slept in
lodging-houses, which were the nests of every
abomination that the mind of man can conceive.   Two hundred and fifty confessed that
they lived together by begging.   Seventy were
the children of convicts.   Many of them had
lost one or both parents.

He brought forward the startling fact that
in the previous year there were sixty-two thou-

sand persons taken into custody, of whom twenty-two thousand could neither read nor write, and twenty-eight thousand had no trade, business calling, or occupation whatever. He said:

"These children, bold, pert, and dirty as London sparrows, but pale, feeble, and sadly inferior to them in plumpness, retire for the night, if they retire at all, to all manner of places—under dry arches of bridges and viaducts; under porticoes, sheds, and carts; in sawpits, on staircases, and in the open air. Curious, indeed, is their mode of life.

"I recollect the case of a boy who, during the inclement season of last winter, passed the greater part of his nights in the iron roller of Regent's Park. He climbed every evening over the railings, and crept to his shelter, where he lay in comparative comfort. Human sympathy, however, prevails even in the poorest condition. He invited a companion less fortunate than himself, promising to 'let him into a good thing.' He did so, and it proved a more friendly act than many a similar undertaking in railway shares.

"A large proportion do not recognize the distinctive rights of *meum* and *tuum*. Property appears to them to be only the aggregate of plunder. They hold that everything that is possessed is common stock; that he who gets most is the cleverest fellow, and that everyone has a right to abstract from that stock what he can by his own ingenuity.

"They make little or no secret of their successful operations, cloaking them with euphemistic terms. They 'find' everything, they 'take' nothing. No matter the bulk or quality of the article, it was 'found'—sometimes nearly a side of bacon, just at the convenient time and place. The buyer of these stolen goods has the high-sounding title, 'dealer in marine stores;' and many are the loud and bitter complaints that the dealer in marine stores is utterly dishonest, and has given for the thing but half the price that could be got in the market.

"These children are like tribes of lawless freebooters, bound by no obligations, and utterly ignorant or utterly regardless of social duties. They trust to their skill, and not to their honesty; gain their livelihood by theft, and consider the whole world as their legitimate prey. With them there is no sense of shame; nor is imprisonment viewed as a disgrace. In many instances it has occurred that after a boy has been a short time at one of the Ragged Schools, he suddenly disappears. At the end of a few weeks he comes back to the very spot in the school where he sat when he was last there. The master, going up to him, says, 'My boy, where have you been?' The boy answers, 'Very sorry, sir, I could not come before; but I have had three weeks at Bridewell.'

"Going to prison is with these children the ordinary lot of humanity. They look upon it as a grievous act of oppression, and when they come to school, they speak of it as one gentleman would tell his wrongs to another.

"Fourteen or fifteen of these boys presented themselves one Sunday evening, and
sat down to the lessons; but as the clock
struck they all rose and left, with the exception
of one, who lagged behind. The master took
him by the arm, and said, 'You must not go;
the lesson is not over.' The reply was, 'We
must go to business.' The master inquired,
'What business?' 'Why, do n't you see, it 's
eight o'clock; we must catch them as they
come out of the chapels.'

"A city missionary who had endeared himself to the whole of a wretched district, one
evening put on a new coat, and went, about
dusk, through a remote street. He was in-
stantly marked as a quarry by one of these
rapacious vagabonds. The urchin did not
know him in his new attire, and therefore
without hesitation relieved his pockets of their
contents. The missionary did not discover his
loss, nor the boy his victim, until in his flight
he had reached the end of the street. He then
looked round, and recognized in the distance

his old friend and teacher. He ran back to
him, breathless. 'Hallo,' said he, 'is it you,
Mr. ——? I did n't know you in your new
coat; here 's your handkerchief for you!'

"The affection they entertain for their
teachers is very striking, based on the unhappy
fact that, except for these devoted missionaries, they have never enjoyed the language
of kindness. Two gentlemen were walking
through the neglected district, when one of
them was accosted by the familiar salutation,
'How are you, there?' He turned to look at the
vagabond who had addressed him so familiarly,
and who shrank back with a disappointed face,
and muttered, 'O, I thought you were teacher; if
you had been, I 'd 'a' shaken hands with you.'

"I have been asked, 'What will you do with
these children when you have educated them?'
I reply with a question, 'What will you do if
you neglect to educate them?' They are not
soap-bubbles nor peach-blossoms—things that
can be puffed away with a child's breath.
They are the seeds of future generations, and

the wheat or the tares will predominate, as
Christian principle or ignorant selfishness shall
govern our conduct. With a just appreciation
of their rights and our own duties, we must
raise them to a level on which they run the
course that is set before them, as citizens of
the British Empire and heirs of a glorious immortality."

The proposition which he made to the Government was this : that the Government should
agree to take every year from the Ragged
Schools a number of children—perhaps five
hundred boys and five hundred girls—and
transplant them at the public expense to Her
Majesty's colonies.

He maintained that if it was held out to
these children as a reward of good conduct,
that the children would be eager and glad to
strive for such a prize as a removal from
scenes where everything was painful, to others
where they can enjoy their existence. He declared his conviction that amongst those
guilty and disgusting children were many

thousands who, if opportunities were given them, would walk in all the dignity of honest men and Christian citizens.

A grant of fifteen thousand pounds was made by the Government for the purpose of an experimental trial of the scheme. This was all too small, and Lord Shaftesbury would have found himself crippled for funds if his friends had not made generous contributions. Fortunately, in the course of his life there were many who thought that the greatest good they could do with their money was to place it in the care of Lord Shaftesbury. He always had schemes on hand which needed help.

"And he was like the "Good Bishop" in "Les Miserables," of whom it is said: "When he had money, he visited the poor; and when he had none, he visited the rich."

Every one who knew him, knew that as a trustee of money he was scrupulously exact, and that not a penny intrusted to him would fail to accomplish some direct end. At one time a legacy of fifty thousand pounds was left to him for distribution among charities.

After the first grant, the Government failed to further his emigration among Ragged Schools, and then he was entirely dependent upon private gifts for his great enterprise.

It was a serious disappointment when the Government withdrew its support, especially since there never was an effort attended with greater success. Testimony came from many sources as to the conduct and efficiency of the Ragged School boys who were sent out to the colonies.

Some lord, who undoubtedly had voted against a grant of funds for emigration, spoke of these children as belonging to the "dangerous classes." To this, Lord Shaftesbury responded with fierce indignation: "Talk of the dangerous classes, indeed! The dangerous classes in England are not the people! They are the lazy ecclesiastics, of whom there are thousands, and the rich who do no good with their money! I fear them more than whole battalions of Chartists!"

The children were carefully selected and specially trained, and each was impressed with the idea that he was to go forth as the representative of a large reserve. Before each detachment started, Lord Shaftesbury visited them, and "some of his farewell addresses on the eve of their departure are worthy of being written in letters of gold, so full are they of tender fatherliness and Christian love."

His biographer has recorded one:

"I see you now, my boys, probably for the last time. You are going to a land where much will depend upon yourselves as regards your future prosperity and success. I hope when you are far away, you will not forget your friends here. The remembrance may, in time of temptation, deter you from doing that which would disgrace yourselves, and bring discredit on them.

"Especially, let me tell you, boys, that however you may rise in the world (and there

is no reason why you should not rise) you
must still be working men. Christianity is not
a speculation; it is essentially practical. You
have something to do for others as well as for
yourselves. You must not, by any misconduct
of yours, bring disgrace upon those who have
gone out before you. Many of those lads who
are now roaming about the streets, houseless
and friendless, may be helped or hindered in
their future course by your conduct. If there
is one single thing more than another which
tends to make a man feel great, it is that he is
answerable for his own conduct to God and
to society at large. Whatever your duty or
circumstances may be, *never forget prayer*.
You may rise to high stations; they are open
to you. Whatever worldly success may be
yours, still, my lads, never forget that the
greatest ambition of the Christian is to be a
citizen of that city whose builder and maker is
God."

In consequence of his speech in the House
of Commons, Lord Shaftesbury entered into

a unique and exceedingly interesting experience in connection with London thieves.
There was a city missionary, named Thomas
Jackson, who had been appointed to the Rag
Fair and Rosemary Lane District, where he
was known as the Thieves' Missionary. They
took him into their confidence; they went to
his house day or night when they needed advice or consolation. He knew more about the
habits of pickpockets, burglars, and every
form of convicted or unconvicted roguery
than the most skillful policemen. He became
a very valuable guide to Lord Shaftesbury, as
well as a very close friend.

Soon after Lord Shaftesbury's speech, in
which he set forth his emigration plan, it occurred to him to ask a notorious adult thief
whether he would like to avail himself of such
a scheme. "I should jump at it," was the
reply. Thus encouraged, he had the same
question proposed at one of Mr. Jackson's
meetings, where the audience was composed
entirely of discharged criminals.

"It would be a capital thing for chaps like us," was their unanimous answer.

Then one of them arose, and proposed that they should write Lord Shaftesbury a letter on behalf of themselves and all their tribe, extending an invitation to him to meet them, and give them his opinion, and advise as to how they could extricate themselves from their present position.

A formal petition was accordingly prepared and sent to Lord Shaftesbury, asking him to meet them. It was signed by forty of the most notorious thieves and burglars of London.

A date was arranged, and without hesitation Lord Shaftesbury accepted the invitation and went. Although he was accustomed to unusual assemblies, he acknowledged that he was not prepared for the strange sight which met his gaze.

There in a large room were four hundred men of every appearance, from the "swell-mob" in black coats and white neckcloths, to the most fierce-looking, **rough**, half-dressed savages he had ever seen.

They had stationed at the door several of the best known and experienced thieves to prevent the admission of any but thieves. There was a little suspicion about some four or five individuals, and they were called forward and put through an examination, in which they proved beyond a doubt that they were members of the dishonest fraternity. The reason for this caution, they explained, was to find out if there was any one there who would betray them.

Lord Shaftesbury was received with genuine enthusiasm, and, having taken the chair, *he opened the meeting by devotional exercises!*

He was anxious to know in which departments of roguery his audience belonged. Some of them were exceedingly well dressed. But many of them had no stockings, and some of them had no shirts. The missionary announced: "His lordship wants to know the particular character of the men here. You

who live by burglary and the more serious
crimes will go to the right, and the others will
go to the left."

About two hundred of the men at once
rose and went to the right, as confessed burglars and living by the greatest crimes.

Lord Shaftesbury then addressed them, and
declared his willingness to befriend them. He
proposed that they should tell him about
themselves. A number of the men then spoke,
and Lord Shaftesbury declared:

"Anything more curious, more graphic,
more picturesque, and more touching I never
heard in my life. They told the whole truth
without the least difficulty, and knowing that
they were there to reveal their condition, they
disguised nothing. I had recommended a re-
linquishing of their old practices, and new re-
solves for the future. 'But how,' said one of
the men, 'are we to live till our next meeting?
We must either steal or die.' "

It was an awkward question. Lord
Shaftesbury acknowledged that he had never

felt so utterly impressed with the magnitude of the task. He confessed that when Jackson urged them "to pray, as God could help them," he felt a certain amount of sympathy when one of the men arose, and with great earnestness said: "My Lord and Gentlemen of the Jury, prayer is very good, but it won't fill an empty stomach!" And at once there arose a general response of "Hear! hear!"

Lord Shaftesbury was sure of one thing. These men were dissatisfied with the life they were leading, and wanted to know how to break away from it. Every one of them was enthusiastic concerning his emigration scheme, and he promised them that he would do all he could for them. They asked him, "But will you ever come back to see us again?" "Yes," he answered, "at any time and at any place, whenever you shall send for me." As he said this, a low, deep murmur of gratitude went round the room.

The result of that night's work can never be estimated. Within three months from that date thirteen who were at that meeting were starting life afresh in Canada, and a little later nearly three hundred of those professional thieves had emigrated, or had passed into different employments, and had no need to return to the old dishonest life.

Lord Shaftesbury had a friend who was a banker, and of whom he was wont to speak as "a prince in the Israel of God." This generous man furnished the funds which made possible the emigration of these men who so sorely needed help in the right direction.

Lord Shaftesbury had learned that the Government knew no gratitude. One of his keen disappointments came in connection with his labors on the Board of Health. It will be remembered that he had rendered services of untold value, involving great personal sacrifice, during the cholera panic. This was but a small item of his work. In every particular he looked after the sanitation of the city.

The *Times* had declared: "To purify the Inferno that reeks about us in this metropolis is

one of the labors to which Lord Shaftesbury
has devoted his life; and we can never be suffi-
ciently obliged to him for undertaking a task
which, besides its immediate disagreeableness,
associates his name with so much that is
shocking and repulsive. To his legislation we
owe the gratifying fact that lodging-houses
are explored by authorized persons, and that
ventilation, lighting, and drainage are provided for. To change a city from clay to
marble is nothing, compared with a trans-
formation from dirt, misery, and vice to clean-
liness, comfort, and at least a decent morality."

Nevertheless, when "the unpardonable activity" of the Board had brought it into col-
lision with the undertakers and water commissioners and sewer agents, the great newspaper
went over to their side.

It soon became apparent that the Board of
Health must be disbanded, and that some
cold, idle, comfortless, do-little office would
be set up in its stead. It was a positive grief
to Lord Shaftesbury, who declared sadly: "I

have given six years of hard labor, and have
not received even the wages of a pointer, with
'that 's a good dog.' We have left no arrears
of business. And thus closes six years of gra-
tuitous and intense labor. I may say with old
George III on the admission of American Independence, 'It may possibly turn out well for
the country, but as a gentleman I can never
forget it!' ''

In a great speech which he made on Sanitary Science, he said:

"When people say that we should think
more of the soul and less of the body, my answer is, that the same God who made the soul
made the body also. It is an inferior work
perhaps, but nevertheles it is his work, and it
must be treated and cared for according to
the end for which it was formed—fitness for
his service. I maintain that God is worshiped,
not only by the spiritual, but by the material
creation. You find it in the Psalms: 'Praise
him, sun and moon; praise him, all ye stars
of light.' And that worship is shown in the

perfection and obedience of the thing made. Our object should be, to do all we can to remove the obstructions which stand in the way of such worship, and of the body's fitness for its great purpose."

In 1872 he laid the foundation-stone of a workman's city, called by his own name, Shaftesbury Park. It was a town on all the modern principles of sanitary arrangements, with recreation grounds, clubs, schools, libraries, and baths. It contained twelve hundred houses, and accommodated eight thousand people.

On his own estate, Wimborne St. Giles, he built a model village, where the cottages were furnished with all the appliances of civilized life, and each had its allotment of a quarter of an acre, the rent being only a shilling a week.

Chapter X

AMONG the interesting experiences into which Lord Shaftesbury entered, none were more so than his acquaintance and friendship with the costers. We find the first outgoings of his heart in this direction, in a book for which he wrote the Preface:

"The pursuit of knowledge under difficulties has always been praised, and justly so; but why should not the pursuit of an honest livelihood amid great temptations be alike admired? Both are great moral efforts; but I am inclined to think that the poor, painstaking costermonger, proof against enticements to fraud and falsehood, is, on the whole, the better citizen of the two. Literature may adorn a nation, but the uprightness of its citizens is its bulwark."

What is a coster? Johnson's Dictionary defined the term thus, "A costermonger is a person who sells apples." But one of the profession indignantly repudiated this definition, and gave a more complete one: "A coster is a cove wot works werry 'ard for a werry poor livin', and is always a-bein' hinterfered with, and blowed up, and moved hon, and fined, and sent to quod by the beaks and bobbies."

A Mr. Orsman, a man holding a humble position in Government service, started the mission. He was attracted to the large population of costers who herded by thousands in an area about Golden Lane. He determined to devote his leisure time to the work of evangelizing them, and established a mission, which very soon had a valuable friend in the person of Lord Shaftesbury.

It was a great day for Mr. Orsman and his work when he received this letter:

"DEAR SIR,—You seem to be engaged in a grand work for the benefit of the poorest classes of the metropolis. The secretary of the Ragged School Union calls it 'a noble work.'

I shall be very glad to aid, so far as I can, such
admirable efforts; and if it can be of any use,
to accept the office of president.

"Your obedient servant,

"SHAFTESBURY."

Mr. Orsman found the costers to be care-
less, improvident, merry, and thoughtless,
with little religion and less politeness. Street
life necessarily cultivated coarseness of language and manners. At night the donkey,
the children, the fathers, and mothers all hud-
dle together in the same room. The stock of
fish, fruit, or vegetables is stored under the
filthy bedsteads, to be carried out the next day
and sold on the streets. They must go to
market very early in summer, and as soon as it
is light in winter, purchasing the cheapest
stock when there is an over-supply, or a better
article which has been cheapened by remaining too long on hand. Their profit is very
small, and their patronage is in the poorer
streets. It was discovered that many of them

made their best profit by using false weights and measures.

Lord Shaftesbury could n't blame them so much for this, when he learned that they were themselves the victims of injustice. Although their capital was small, it was generally borrowed at a most exorbitant rate of interest from money lenders, who took advantage of the necessities of the poor fellows. Lord Shaftesbury became a sort of banker for the concern, loaning them money at small interest, and encouraging them to deal to others as they would be dealt by.

He showed, in his speeches, how useful these costers are to the people, as they bring to the door of the working classes cheap fruit, fish, and vegetables, which otherwise they could not get, being too far from the country, and not being able to patronize the large markets. Their income was most uncertain, depending on the weather and the chance of over-supply. Like all such people, they were very improvident, and knew what it was to suffer with hunger through the long winter. Their highest ambition was to own a donkey and a truck. Most of them were too poor to have their own, and rented by the day or week.

From the beginning of his knowledge of these people, Lord Shaftesbury took the liveliest interest in them. He always delighted to call himself a "coster," and nothing would induce him to lose an opportunity of spending a social evening with his "brethren."

He organized a Barrow and Donkey Club, and enrolled himself as a member. This made it necessary for him to buy a barrow and donkey, which he would loan to those who were unfortunate. The barrow was a handsome one, and bore upon it the Shaftesbury arms and motto. Happy and proud was the coster who had the loan of these precious pieces of property.

He had it in his power to help them in important directions. For example, the vestry of St. Luke's Church issued an order forbidding costermongers to trade any longer in Whitecross Street. As this was a profitable district, the costers were alarmed for their interests. Lord Shaftesbury made a plea before the parish magistrates, and they at once withdrew their order.

At one of the meetings Lord Shaftesbury told the men that if at any time they had grievances which he might be able to redress, they should write him, and he would answer promptly.

"But where shall we send our letters?" asked one. "Address your letter to me at Grosvenor Square, and it will reach me," he replied; "but if after my name you put 'K. G. and Coster,' there will be no doubt that I shall get it."

Did ever England's proud order know such a combination as *Knight of the Garter and Coster!*

It was proverbial that the donkeys were shamefully ill-used. Lord Shaftesbury was president of the Society for the Prevention of

Cruelty to Animals, and at once he set about improving the condition of the patient little beasts. He had tests made to show how much better work they could do if they rested on Sunday. He instituted donkey shows, where he gave a prize to the coster whose donkey gave evidence of the best care.

It was no uncommon thing to see him stop in the street to salute a coster and pat his donkey, and commend its appearance and ask how business was going.

One day Lord Shaftesbury received an invitation from the costers to meet them in their hall, where they wished to make him a presentation. He went, and took the president's chair as usual. Over a thousand costers with their friends were present, and with surprising thoughtfulness some ladies and gentlemen had been invited, and were there on the platform. A handsome donkey, extravagantly decorated with ribbons, was led on to the platform, and presented to Lord Shaftesbury. He at once vacated the chair, and made way for the new arrival. And then, putting his arm around the animal's neck, he thanked them in a short speech. He said: "When I have passed away from this life, I desire to have no more said of me than that I have done my duty, as the poor donkey has done his, with patience and unmurmuring resignation."

The donkey was then led down the steps of the platform, and Lord Shaftesbury remarked: "I hope the reporters of the press will state that, the donkey having vacated the chair, the place was taken by Lord Shaftesbury!"

The donkey was sent to St. Giles, where he was a great pet. Its death is thus recorded:

"DEAR ORSMAN,—I am grieved to say that Coster is no more. He broke away from the stable, and made a dash for the paddock. In so doing, he fell and smashed his thigh. The veterinary surgeon was sent for, who pronounced him incurable, and advised that he should be put out of his pain.

"The friendly and useful creature was

buried with all honors in a place I have within
a thick plantation, where the pet dogs and
horses that have served the family and deserved our gratitude are gathered together.

"Remember me very warmly to my brother
costermongers, their wives, and their children.

"SHAFTESBURY."

The costers sent another to supply his
place, and of him Shaftesbury wrote:

"DEAR ORSMAN,—The brown donkey has
won the affection of every one. My grand-
children declare it is the most attractive, amiable creature they ever knew. It follows
them like a spaniel.

"Give my love to the costers, and say how
happy I would be to meet them again.

"What day will suit my brother costers for
the show?   Yours,   S."

His journal has many references to the
costers:

"A wonderful meeting in Golden Lane last

night. A spectacle to gladden angels—comfort, decency, education, and spiritual life, in the midst of filth, destitution, vice, and misery. This work of the gospel is administered by a clerk in the post-office, who gives all his spare time and the most of his money to advance the knowledge of Christ, and the earthly and heavenly interests of man. It was enough to humble me. Few things are more marvelous than to see what can be done by one man, whatever his social position, if he have but the love of Christ in his heart, and the grace of our Lord to lead him on."

"February 28th.—I went with Orsman through Golden Lane to visit my costermongers. Well do these poor people put us all to shame. Piety, resignation, faith, in the depths of penury, and seemingly without hope.

"On the 5th I went to Orsman's tea-party of aged costers in Golden Lane—poor old dears! Had to give them a 'hortation,' as Hobbes translates Thucydides."

Although he knew so many people, they were not known to him as a class; but he remembered the individual—their particular needs and circumstances. We see this in extracts from letters to Mr. Orsman:

"Do you ever perambulate your district by day? If so, I should like to accompany you."

"Do not forget the woman who made the braces. We promised her something. I have sent two copies of the 'Faithful Promiser' for the two wives of the cabinetmaker and the old paralyzed man."

"Your missionaries must talk to the poor cabinetmaker, and pray with him. He is not hardened. Let him have what he wants in his necessity."

"I have sent you a book for the two sons of the spectacle-woman and the paralytic husband. Also picture cards, as I promised, to the little girl who is daughter of the shoemaker's wife, who went security for a watercress girl."

Thus he entered into their lives with fullest

13

sympathy, and we must remember that the costers were but one class of the many for whom he thought and worked and suffered.

One night he went from the House of Lords to a devotional service held by the costers. He contrasted these two places in a way which showed where his heart was.

He speaks of the House of Lords as "that vast aquarium full of cold-blooded life," and then he alludes tenderly to the simple-hearted piety and loving hearts which he found in the costers' prayer-meeting.

He regarded the costers' mission as one of the happiest successes of all the movements with which he had been identified. And he was especially gratified that the costers' kind treatment of their donkeys had led to a universal improvement in the care of beasts of burden all over London.

In 1875, after the greatest sorrow of his life, the death of his wife, he turned his thought toward the watercress and flower girls of the great city. In memory of his wife he estab-

lished a fund, which he named the Emily Loan
Fund. It was a scheme to enable these poor
girls, whose battle with life is very hard, to
earn their living when watercress and flowers
are out of season.

Lord Shaftesbury placed in the hands of
the committee of the mission a sum of money,
from which deserving applicants might draw,
to enable them to purchase stock-in-trade for
the winter. Poor women came in companies,
and made application for the loan of baked-
potato ovens, coffee stalls, barrows, and
boards.

The condition upon which the loans were
granted was, that borrowers must find security for the full value of the article, thereby pro-
tecting the fund from loss, and giving the best
guarantee of the honesty and industry of the
borrower. When the value of the article was
repaid, it became the property of the hirer.
Lord Shaftesbury said: "I believe that among
these watercress girls there are many as honest
and as pure as are to be found in all London.

Those who are successful go into business, and often buy a coffee-stall, the outfit for which costs as much as ten pounds."

He was one day at the office of the superintendent of the mission, when a nice-looking girl came in. She said:

"I want a loan, please, of a very large sum."

"What for, my dear?"

"For flowers and basket."

"Have you anything in the world?"

"Not a sixpence."

"Can you give security?"

"O yes! the shoemaker's wife will go bail for me."

"How much do you want?"

"Well, I do n't think I can do with a penny less than one pound."

It was given, and every farthing was repaid.

The girls change their business with the seasons. They are fruit girls in summer, flower girls in spring, coffee-stall keepers in winter.

Lord Shaftesbury declared that it was the

most successful loan establishment in all London. They had out a thousand loans, and did not lose fifty pounds during the whole period. Not in a single instance did they have to recover by legal means. The little that was lost was by reason of sickness or death, and not by fraud.

One of the side activities of the Ragged School movement was the cultivation of plants and flowers under certain regulations by the scholars. On a given day they were all brought together in a large hall, and at this flower show prizes were awarded for the plants which showed the best care.

" The advantages of these flower shows in a social aspect were many. They provided a source of simple recreation, and gave a new interest in home by adding unwonted cheerfulness to the comfortless rooms of the poor. They became the means of drawing attention to some of the social wants of the working classes, such as the need of fresh air and ventilation and more space. They taught them

simple habits of forethought and prudence;
for if they would win the prizes, they must
purchase their plants long beforehand. Their
chief good was that in watching the growth
and progress of the flowers under their care
the children and their parents were brought
into close contact with something pure and
innocent—something that should speak to the
better part of their natures, and tell them of
Him who has made the earth beautiful.

"It seemed almost incredible that many of
the plants and flowers exhibited at these shows
were reared and watched and tended in some
close cellar or garret by the little ragged
urchins, who, a short time before, were whin-
ing in the street for alms."

The flowers, humble and simple enough,
breathed whispers of strange histories. Some
were reared in crowded slums, where the
owner stole a few minutes from the hardest
toil to tend them. Some came from Westminster Hospital, where they had been cared
for by sick and suffering children. Some were

sent from the Cripples' Home, and some from the kitchens of domestic servants and the quiet homes of working people.

Dean Stanley was the president of this Society for Promoting Flower Culture, but Lord Shaftesbury always gave the prizes at the annual flower show. He used to tell with great pleasure a little incident that occurred on one of these occasions.

As he was going about among the people, he felt a little hand slip into his, and a little girl looked up in his face, and said, "Please, sir, may I give you a kiss?" The loving-hearted Earl smiled down into the little pinched face, and answered heartily, "I am sure you may, my dear, and I'll give you one, too." In speaking of it, he said, "What would London be without her children?"

The year of his great sorrow he wrote Dean Stanley, saying that he had better find some new and younger chairman for the annual flower show, and adding that he was in the condition of a tree which, as Lucan says, "casts a shadow no longer with its leaves, but only by its stem."

Dean Stanley replied with the following verses:

> "Well said old Lucan, Often have I seen
> A stripling tree, all foliage and all green,
> But not a hope of grateful, soothing shade;
> Its empty strength in fluttering leaves displayed.
> Give me the solid trunk, the aged stem,
> That rears its scant but glorious diadem;
> That, through long years of battle or of storm,
> Has striven whole forests round it to reform;
> That plants its roots too deep for man to shake;
> That lifts its head too high for grief to break;
> That still, thro' lightning-flash and thunder-stroke,
> Retains its vital sap and heart of oak;
> Such gallant tree for me shall ever stand,
> A great rock's shadow in a weary land."

Lord Shaftesbury wrote under this: "I knew that the dean was very kindly disposed towards me. But I did not know how kindly."

He withdrew his resignation and attended the show, where he made the most fervent address he had ever given to these people, whom he loved so tenderly.

Chapter XI

WE have given but small attention to the personal and home life of this great man. That he was very often drawn away from the delights of his own circle by the many calls of his public life was a constant grief. Only the conviction that he was called to this sacred work for the poor and neglected children of men kept him in the slums and missions of the great city, when his own home was the spot in all the world where most he wished to be. When he placed his eldest son at school, we find him writing:

"Dear Antony is about to start for school. How can I let him go! He is such a joy to me! Well can I understand the gracious and precious wisdom that shone in the hearts of Josiah and King Edward. O God, make him like Samuel, to walk before thee in youth and in age with joyful obedience!"

When he goes to get him to bring him home for his first vacation, he is as happy as a child. He says:

"I took Minny with me, and also Francis, Maurice, and Evelyn. Very expensive; but we had incautiously made the promise. Children hold much to such engagements; and the loss of money is of less account than the loss of confidence."

When he was obliged to leave his little flock his heart staid behind. He says:

"My heart misgave me as I saw baby straining her darling little face through the bars of the pier to get a last sight of me. I commit my little flock unto God and the word of his grace."

When he decided in favor of Rugby instead of Eton as a school for his son, he gave his reason thus:

"Eton fits a man beyond all competition for the drawing-room, the club, St. James Street, and all the mysteries of social elegance. But it does not make the man required for

the coming generation. We must have
nobler, deeper, and sterner stuff; more of the
inward, not so much of the outward gentleman; a just estimate of rank and property as
gifts from God, bringing with them serious
responsibilities."

In the fall of 1846 Ireland was on the brink
of starvation. Lord Shaftesbury maintained
that every one ought, by private self-denial, to
aid the legislative effort for relief and lessen
his own consumption, that "all might have a
little." He was one of the first to practice his
own preaching. When he found all provisions
rising in price, he gave orders that no more
potatoes should be bought for the house, saying: "We must not, by competing in the market, raise the cost on the poor man. He has
nothing after this to fall back upon."

An impression prevailed, that because Lord
Shaftesbury had succeeded to the earldom,
and possessed large landed estates, he must, of
necessity, be possessed of wealth. The fact is,
that his financial difficulties were often most

distressing.   As the head of a noble house
which must be maintained, and as the father
of ten children who must be educated and
cared for, he found his income all too small.
And yet these were not the largest items in his
expense account.

His biographer says that "heroism" is not
too large a word to use with reference to the
long, hard battle he fought in his endeavor to
obey the apostolic injunction, and "to owe no
man anything."

As a leader in every charitable organization of the day he could not urge liberal giving
upon others, and not give freely himself.   The
demands upon his private charity were almost
incredible in number and extent.   When Lord
Shaftesbury put his name down on a subscrip-
tion-list, he offered to God that which cost
him self-denial, self-sacrifice, and anxiety.

A lady called on him one day, and brought
to his attention a distressing case—a Polish
refugee, who was in a state of utter destitution.

"Dear me!" he said, "what is to be done?

I have not a farthing. But the poor fellow must have something at once. What can I do?"

He was as distressed as though some strong personal trouble had come to him. Suddenly a happy thought seized him. He remembered that he had put away in his library a five-pound note in reserve as a nest-egg, and bringing it in with an air of great delight, he asked his visitor to relieve the man's distress as soon as possible.

We find these records in his journal:

"I have made up my mind that I must sell the old family pictures and the old family estates. It is painful, because ancestral feelings are very strong with me. But it is far better to have a well-cottaged property, people in decency and comfort, than well-hung walls which persons seldom see, and almost never admire unless pressed to do so; and as for estates, it is ruin to retain them in the face of mortgage, debt, and the necessary provision for my children!

"To-day I sent to St. Giles for two more pictures to be sold. The house must be repaired, and I must not do it from any revenue by which moneys devoted to charity would be diverted. I must, therefore, surrender my heirlooms, dismantle my walls, check ancestral feeling, and thank God that it is no worse."

It seems incredibly sad that a man of Lord Shaftesbury's ability and benevolence should have had financial embarrassments. Fortunately, he had a friend in Lord Palmerston, the Premier of England, who had married his mother-in-law, and who ventured to ask him if his agents were trustworthy, and if, in his laudable desire to improve every part of his estate, he had not trusted his manager to devote a larger portion of his income than should have been allotted for such a purpose.

The inquiry came none too soon. The extent of Lord Shaftesbury's losses were never fully known, but were probably not less than fifty thousand pounds.

For many years he was to have trouble and

anxiety without ceasing, endless lawsuits and
vexations. Things were at their worst, when
Palmerston sent to Lord Shaftesbury's wife
five thousand pounds, stating that he must be
allowed to pay his half "of his son's start in the
world."

This generous gift was truly appreciated,
and gave the temporary help which was sorely
needed. The dread of debt was a horror of
great darkness before him. He wrote to a
friend: "If I appear to fail in life and vigor, it
is not for the want of zeal, but from that kind
of Promethean eagle that is ever gnawing at
my vitals. May God be with you and keep
you *out of debt!*"

Had he been a man of less determination
and courage, he would have abandoned his
great undertakings, overwhelmed with his personal obligations. Not so, Lord Shaftesbury.
He entered more heartily than ever into the
work to which he had given his life.

His journal of this time says:

"Engaged more than ever. Small works

compared with the political and financial
movements of the day—a Lodging-house, a
Ragged School, a Vagrant Bill, a Thieves'
Refuge! No wonder that people think me
engaged in small work, and yet I would not
change it. Surely God has called me to this
career.

"I imagine some young man saying to me,
'Would you counsel me to follow the career
that you have chosen and pursued?' I reply
that, in spite of all vexations, disappointments,
rebuffs, insults, toil, expense, weariness, all
loss of political position, and considerable loss
of personal estimation; in spite of being always secretly despised and often publicly ig-
nored; in spite of having your 'evil' most ma-
liciously exaggerated, and your 'good' evil
spoken of,—I would for myself say, 'Yes.' If
you desire to rise in the world, to have a party,
to be much thought of, to be a great man at
court or in politics, I should say, 'No.' If you
desire internal satisfaction, that humble joy
through Almighty God that will attend you

in retirement and thoughtfulness, I say emphatically, 'Yes.'"

In a letter to his intimate friend, Mr. Haldane, he said:

"When I was younger I had some ambition for myself; I have now no desire except to possess so much influence as may enable me to do good. The public grows weary of its servants; it is tired of 'humanity,' and dead sick of *me*. Whether by being out of sight for a time I shall come forth like an old coat with a new fluff, is a matter of speculation. I much fear that they will find me out, and as the showman said to Lord Stowell, when he went to see the mermaid, 'You have been a customer to me, my Lord, and I'll not take you in; it is only the old monkey!' So they will say, 'Don't attend to that speech, it's only the old monkey!'"

On one occasion when he went into the committee rooms of the House of Lords, he heard one of the members say: "What! are we not to have any new speakers, none but the

14

old ones?" Lord Shaftesbury said: "He blurted out, not at all in an intentionally offensive spirit, a sad truth. The guilt and punishment of thirty years of platform work rushed upon my conscience. But I was obliged to proceed."

He felt very keenly the abuse of the newspapers. When he was advocating open-air services for the poor people, the *Daily News* called him "an obtrusive professor of street-corner piety," and added that "the Pharisaism of Lord Shaftesbury is unimpeached and unimpeachable!"

He said: "A great majority of mankind assume that if a man be stamped as a 'philanthropist,' he can not have common sense. They hold that it betokens a softening of the brain! Alas! poor Yorick!"

He was one of the most overworked men in all the great city. At the beginning of the year 1849 we find him laying out this program for himself:

"I must stir up the Board of Health to

more vigorous efforts. One hundred and fifty children have recently died of proved neglect. They will be the martyrs of a cause of reformation. Next, I must carry out my plan for the general subdivision of all the larger parishes, so that the population of each parish shall not exceed four thousand, a plan that I feel sure will effect a greater amount of moral, social, and religious improvement than a whole code of laws. Then the completion of Ragged School projects, especially in relation to emigration. And, finally, the invitation to the stragglers in the lanes and streets, and the arrangement for evangelistic services in the great theaters. Add to this the ordinary and existing work, and there is my budget!"

Before many months had passed, he began to have most unpleasant symptoms—terrible noises in his ears, his whole body appearing to vibrate like a Jew's-harp. He consulted a physician, and sorrowfully records his verdict:

"Over-toil, over-anxiety, over-sensitiveness to the subjects handled during many years, have unnerved you completely. You must be more moderate, or utterly disabled."

After a brief rest, he writes:

"I am harassed by letters, interviews, chairs, boards, speeches. I am worn, worn by them all, surrendering all amusements and society, giving all the day and half of almost every night to business and meetings, and all this in the face of weak health and tottering nerves."

When it was rumored that he was very ill, four hundred poor people called at his door in a single day to inquire about him. This touched him deeply, as the sincere attentions of humble people always did.

After he had passed the threescore and ten milestone, his activity knew no cessation. There was scarcely a social, political, or religious movement set on foot in which his coöperation was not solicited, and, if possible, obtained.

He said at one of the meetings of the Ragged School Union: "This is the ninth hour I have been in the chair to-day. Moreover, I have taken the chair for two and thirty years consecutively, and having made two and thirty speeches, I hardly know in what form to address you."

It is to be regretted that more of Lord Shaftesbury's speeches were not preserved, to take a permanent place in the literature of the country. Not alone because of their literary value, but because they are the utterances of a man intensely in earnest, who had thoroughly mastered every subject he discussed.

It was a great pleasure to Lord Shaftesbury that his wife and children entered heartily into his plans and partook of his spirit.

When his son Evelyn wrote to congratulate him on the success of one of his great speeches, he replied:

"God bless you, my darling boy, for your kind and sympathizing letter. The success was indeed wonderful. You ask me how I get through so much work; why, as I hope you will hereafter, by hearty prayer to Al-

mighty God before I begin, by entering into
it with faith and zeal, and by making my end
to be his glory and the good of mankind."

We find this record in his journal of 1860:

"Last season in London my four daughters
attended twice a week at the Cripples' Hospital to amuse the little, helpless ones, and
read to them. It was signally successful, and
blessed by God's grace to the teachers and the
taught. Never have I felt more joy than to
see that the more wretched the object, the
more degraded and helpless the sufferer, the
greater the sympathy of my children, and the
greater their devotion. 'Every good and perfect gift cometh down from above!'"

The first great sorrow of his life was the
death of his second son, Francis, who sickened
and died at Harrow, where he had made a
most remarkable record as a student. He,
perhaps more than any other child, was like
his father in temperament, religious fervor,
and philanthropic spirit. His father reached
him in time to give him his blessing, and to

assure him that he had the prayers of hundreds of ragged children. His face kindled at the thought, and it seemed to please him most of all. Lord Shaftesbury alludes to it thus:

"Yesterday, at eight o'clock in the evening, it pleased Almighty God to take our blessed Francis. It was the work of a moment, and we were like amazed persons, so great had been the promise not many seconds before of returning strength. Yet we must not murmur, for all is wisdom and mercy and love that cometh from Him. The child is with Christ, which is far better. When the physician told him he could not live, he simply added, 'Whatever is God's will, is enough for me.'"

For many months there is scarcely a page of his journal that does not record the name of "my blessed Francis." His portrait was on the mantelpiece in the study at St. Giles; and thirty-six years later Lord Shaftesbury declared his belief that not one day had passed without some conscious memory of his beloved son.

Within a week of the funeral we find him busy with his Ragged Schools. He says a new motive impelled him:

"Work of the 'Ragged' kind recalls his image so vividly, and his dear words of sympathy and approval. How could I please him more, were he here, or if he knows of my doings, than by seeking the welfare of these forlorn lambs of our Master?"

His son Maurice became the victim of a malady which affected his intellect, and finally terminated his life. Lord Shaftesbury had for him a feeling of peculiar tenderness. He said:

"Wonderful it is that this feeble boy had such a charm about him. I have directed a monument on which will be engraved two texts which he cherished and often repeated: 'The Lord is my Shepherd, I shall not want;' 'It is good for me that I have been afflicted.' How good, he now knows in reality; he knew it before by faith. Frequently in speaking and in writing I have been permitted to comfort him by quoting the words of our blessed Lord,

'What I do thou knowest not now, but thou shalt know hereafter.'

"I have lost two precious sons for the short time of human life; but I have housed them forever in heaven."

In 1861 his darling daughter, Mary, after an illness of a year and a half, died with consumption. He speaks of the beautiful love between mother and daughter, which grew stronger as the invalid grew weaker: "The mother's devotion to the child, and the child's affection for the mother, are God's own gifts."

In 1857, Lord Shaftesbury's eldest son, Antony, was elected to the House of Commons from Hull. He writes:

"It was accomplished without a bribe, treating, or any illicit inducement. His success is wonderful, and is of God's goodness. May it be the beginning of a career noble, patriotic, useful, religious, to his Master's honor and man's welfare! Evelyn was there, and showed every quality of a clever, energetic man of business."

At a public dinner given to his son, Lord Shaftesbury said:

"You have taken that youth by the hand, and started him in the race of life with every hope of usefulness and honor. It is a matter of deep emotion that I should now see my son, in his earliest years, placed in that position where many men have terminated their career; that I see him commencing life in the highest situation that British freemen can confer upon their fellow-citizens; that I see him intrusted with mighty interests, and the member for the third seaport in the kingdom."

When the first grandson was born, he wrote a joyful letter to his friend Haldane:

"My little village of St. Giles is all agog with the birth of a son and heir in the very midst of them, the first, it is believed, since about 1600, when the first Lord Shaftesbury was born. The christening yesterday was an ovation. Every cottage had flags and flowers. We had three triumphal arches, and all the people were exulting. 'He is one of us.' 'He

is a fellow-villager.' The tenants, too, and
clergy, have, in grand consultation, resolved
to present a piece of plate as an heirloom. I
doubt whether in many counties there would
now be found such a feeling between the
owner and the occupiers of the land. Much
is due to Antony, who has lived among them,
and made himself deservedly popular."

We have seen how little this great man
cared for the honors of the world, although he
did care very much for the good-will of those
whom he believed to be true and good,
whether in high or lowly life.

When the chancellorship of Oxford was
made vacant by the death of the Duke of
Wellington, and Shaftesbury was approached
as to whether he would receive it, he said:

"It would, of necessity, call me away from
the duties I have undertaken. Is there one
that I would surrender for this honor? Not
one. It is an honor I do not covet, a comfortless dignity. Let those who are ambitious
for it, obtain and enjoy the post. There will

be candidates enough. I had rather, by God's blessing and guidance, retain those places for which there are *no candidates*—the presidency of the Ragged School, the Field Lane Refuge. This is clearly my province. I am called to this, and not to any political or social honors."

In 1854, when he was fighting battles for chimney-sweepers, and for the kings of the east, and in behalf of Ragged Schools and sanitation and pure literature, he received the following letter from the Prime Minister:

"MY DEAR SHAFTESBURY,—It would give me great pleasure if you would permit me to submit your name to the Queen for the vacant Blue Ribbon. This is not intended as a political appointment; for although I hope your general feelings are not unfriendly to the Government, I make the proposal exclusively from 'a desire to mark my admiration of your unwearied exertions in the cause of humanity and of social improvement.

"I am aware that honors of this description
are usually conferred from very different motives; but I feel certain that the distinction
was never better deserved, and I doubt not
that I shall myself receive credit for making
such a selection.

"Believe me, very truly yours,

"ABERDEEN."

As was usual with all weighty questions,
Lord Shaftesbury discussed it in his journal:

"May 5th.—Though my immediate impulse was to decline it, I prayed to God for
counsel and guidance. The point to be considered is, 'Will it impede or will it promote
my means of doing good?' Minny wants me
to accept it, 'as a just acknowledgment,' so
she says, 'of my deserts.' I am unwilling to
do so, lest it should be considered a *payment*
of them, and I be told hereafter, either that
I was never disinterested in my labors, or,
when I appeal to Government for aid in my

projects, that they have done enough to oblige me, and that they can do no more! It might lead ignorant or malicious persons to cry down all public virtue, and say that every public man had his price.

"The novelty of this reward for such services as mine would offend many people, and lower the value of the decoration among those for whom it is principally intended.

"And the fees would amount to more than a thousand pounds, a sum which, if I had, I must devote either to my children or to duties towards my people. God give me a true judgment!"

"May 10th.—I have written to Aberdeen, and declined the Garter. But I thanked him heartily and affectionately for his kindness, and for the estimate he put on my public services. He understood my difficulties, and sent my letter to the Queen. I regret the necessity of the determination, for I am not indifferent to the honor; but I am sure that I have done wisely. God be praised!"

A week later he wrote:

"The Government in the House of Commons threw out the Chimney-sweepers' Bill, and said not a word of sympathy for the wretched children, nor of desire to amend the law. I am very sad and low about the loss of the Sweeps Bill. The Collar of the Garter might have choked me. At least, I have not this or any other Government favor against me as an offset to their oppression. I must persevere, and, by God's help, so I will; for, however dark the view, I see no Scripture reason for desisting; and the issue of every toil is in the hands of the Almighty."

As we have seen, this bill was finally passed, and recorded as a victory for Lord Shaftesbury.

In 1855, Lord Palmerston had become Prime Minister, and he offered Shaftesbury the same honor.

"I never was in such perplexity in my life," said Lord Shaftesbury to his friend Hodder. "I was at my wit's end. On one side was ranged wife, relations, friends, ambition, influence; on the other, my own objections, which seemed sometimes to weigh as nothing in comparison with the arguments brought against them. I could not satisfy myself that to accept office was a divine call. I *was* satisfied that God had called me to labor among the poor. There was no Urim and Thummim; no open vision. I could do nothing but postpone, and, in doing this, I was placing Palmerston in a most awkward position. But God interposed for me."

Lord Palmerston was in a dilemma. He had been unable to find any one who would satisfactorily fill the vacancy, otherwise he would have relieved his friend from the pressure that he knew was intolerable. His own light and hopeful spirit made him believe that once in office, all the objections would disappear, and only good would ensue. But had he seen any way of escape for his friend, he would not have continued his urgent demands. A message was sent to Lord Shaftesbury to put on his court dress, and be at the palace at a given hour. To use his own words:

"I never felt so helpless. I seemed to be hurried along without a will of my own; without any power of resistance. I went and dressed, and then, while I was waiting for the carriage, I went down on my knees and prayed for counsel, wisdom, and understanding. Then there was some one at the door, as I thought, to say that the carriage was ready. Instead of that, a note, hurriedly written in pencil, was put into my hands. It was from Palmerston, 'Don't go to the palace.' That was thirty years ago, but I dance with joy at the remembrance of that interposition, as I did when it happened. It was, to my mind, as distinctly an act of special providence as when the hand of Abraham was stayed and Isaac escaped." Another man had been found, who was acceptable to the Queen.

Six years later, Lord Palmerston renewed his offer of this honor, declaring that the nation demanded his acceptance, and that the

15

financial hindrance had been removed. Lord
Shaftesbury's acceptance of the honor is referred to thus:

"Strange to say, I am become a 'Knight of
the Garter.' I could not persist in refusal, so
great was Palmerston's anxiety, and so urgent
his arguments. I wished on many grounds to
avoid the honor; but obstinacy in refusal
would have been almost personal to him, and
misunderstood in myself. I do not despise,
nor would I publicly depreciate, such rewards.
They have their real value. It has been declared to be an acknowledgment of services
hitherto considered to be of no public value.
So far I rejoice.

"How my precious, precious Mary would
have been pleased! But the darling has better
things to please her now.

"Palmerston assured me he had made an
arrangement with the Treasury about the fees,
which amount to about a thousand pounds.
I have reason to believe that the arrangement
he made was to pay the whole expense him-

self, but to keep it secret from me. This is indeed generous."

In the closing years of his life many honors were publicly accorded to him. In 1884 a great banquet was given at the Mansion House, at which he was the guest of the evening. It was a splendid ovation, three hundred persons, representing all the great social, religious, and political interests, responding to the invitation. In June of that year, amid great pomp and circumstance, he received somewhat tardily the freedom of the city of London. In acknowledging the honor, he said that if he could not add any luster to the citizenship, the time for him was so short that there would be little opportunity for him to tarnish it, and added that, if any one should ever undertake the task of writing his biography, he begged him to have the goodness to record that he died a citizen of London.

In 1872 came the great sorrow of his life. There is nothing in all literature more pathetic than the record of his grief.

On the anniversary of his wedding day he had written:

"Forty-one years ago I was united to that dear, beautiful, true, and affectionate darling, my blessed Minny. What a faithful, devoted, simple-hearted, and captivating wife she has been to me! And what a mother! Lord, give me grace to thank thee evermore, and rejoice in thy goodness. Lead us in the way of service. She is still away with my precious, suffering Constance, who is seeking health in a milder climate. God in his mercy, bring them home speedily and safely!"

It was while caring for her invalid daughter that the health of Lady Shaftesbury gave way. As soon as she was able to bear the journey, she returned to London. The physicians declared it a "grave case." In the hour of his overwhelming anxiety Lord Shaftesbury wrote to Mr. Orsman:

"I am writing to you with the very pen my costermonger friends gave me. I write to ask my brothers and sisters in Golden Lane to pray for me. My wife and daughter are very ill. I believe much in the prayers of Christian people; and I know there are many among you. Do not forget me. Our Lord teaches us that there is mighty power in the fervent supplications of the poor. The children, too, must remember me, as I have often remembered them. May God be with you!

"Shaftesbury."

For several days Lady Shaftesbury appeared to be gaining in strength, but there was a serious relapse, and on October 15th we find this record in his journal:

"Minny, my own Minny, is gone. God took her soul to himself at about twelve o'clock this morning. She has entered into her rest, and has left us to feel the loss of the purest, gentlest, kindest spirit that ever lived. O my God, what a blow! But we bow before thee in resignation and sorrow. She whispered to me, 'None but Christ.' What do I not owe to her and to thee, O God, for the gift of her? But now to-night will be a terrible event. For the first time I must omit in my prayers the name of my precious Minny."

Four days later the body of Lady Shaftesbury was committed to the grave in the little village church of Wimborne St. Giles. A simple tablet near the family pew bears a tribute:

"To the memory of a wife, as good, as true, and as deeply beloved as God, in his undeserved mercy, ever gave to man."

Expressions of sympathy poured in upon Lord Shaftesbury from Her Majesty, the Queen, who wrote a most beautiful and tender autograph letter, and from many humble Ragged School teachers, and from a multitude of illiterate costers.

It seemed impossible that Lady Constance Ashley could survive the shock. But she rallied, and her physicians said her only hope was on the shores of the Mediterranean. His record tells of the pathetic struggle for life:

"The doctors say, Mentone; but how get

her there? How find her strength for the long, fatiguing journey? How get her across the water in wind and rain? O God, be gracious to us!

"To-day I went to St. Giles on business. How sad and solitary and silent it is! When it was dark I crept into the church, and prayed near her dear resting-place, and I had peace.

"Mentone.—We arrived here very sorrowful. I could enjoy nothing, for she was not here to share it with me. I must live for Constance's sake. No attention, no sympathy can approach that of a mother—and such a mother!

"December 16th.—To-day my precious Constance left me for heaven. Never was a going so joyous. Heaven itself seemed open before her eyes. Her face was radiant as she spoke to every one. 'Dearest father,' she said, 'I want to bless you now for all that you have taught me.' The darling girl taught me in one half-hour more than I had imparted in her whole life. She said: 'I know that I am

going to die, for I feel so happy.' With these
words she fell into a soft sleep, and was gone.
Was her blessed mother there? She said,
'Christ is very near.' I will ever maintain that
this was a special mercy to mitigate our sorrow. We were positively raised into joy.
Neither speech nor writing can adequately de-
scribe what it was. The sudden change was
like a resurrection."

"December 28th.—Yesterday was the burial. The day was dark and gloomy; but as
we started on the procession, the sun came out
like a smile of heaven."

Whenever he returned to St. Giles, he
seemed to feel his loss and sorrow more
keenly. When his son, the Hon. Evelyn Ashley, was returned as member of Parliament,
the little village held a glad celebration, and
Lord Shaftesbury writes:

"The bells are ringing joyfully; but she, my
beloved one, who lies beneath them, hears
them not. How glad would her dear heart

have been in the success of her sympathizing
son! But she is listening to other sounds—
the music of heaven.

"In her old age she was as beautiful to me
as the day when I married her."

Chapter XII

AS we have seen, Lord Shaftesbury revered the Church of England for the truths which she held, and for what she might be. He acknowledged sorrowfully that her clergy had failed to stand by him in his great work. He was often denounced and opposed by the Establishment because of his broad catholic spirit, which reached out to sympathize and co-operate with every humanitarian effort under whatsoever Church or creed. He declared himself that he was "an Evangelical of the Evangelicals." He requested his biographer, "Do not tone down or explain away my *unpopular religious views.*"

On one occasion, speaking of Church reform, he said:

"I have talked a great deal, always with a view to the safety of the Establishment, about ecclesiastical reforms. Ecclesiastical reforms

seem just as remote as they were before anything was said on the subject. I am not going
to speak about such things any more, and I
will tell you why. Two hundred years ago, an
ancestor of mine, the Lord Shaftesbury of that
day, was making a speech in the House of
Lords. Behind him sat the bishops, and one
of them whose name I find recorded in history, and who disliked the Lord Shaftesbury
of that day, perhaps, nearly as much as the
bishops now dislike the Lord Shaftesbury of
the present day, exclaimed, 'When will that
lord have done preaching?' My ancestor
turned round to him, and said, 'Whenever
your lordships begin.' Well, I will not go on
preaching any more about ecclesiastical reform, because it would be utterly useless, because I know their lordships, the bishops, will
never begin."

He describes a ritualistic service, and closes
with a Scripture verse, which surely is the best
comment which could be made:

"On Sunday I went to St. Alban's Church

in Holborn. In outward form and ritual, it is
the worship of Jupiter and Juno. A high altar,
a cross over it—no end of pictures. The chan-
cel very large, and separated from the body of
the church by a tall iron grille. Service in-
toned and sung, except the lessons, by priests
with white surplices and green stripes.

"This being ended, a sudden clearance. All
disappeared. In a few minutes, the organ, the
choristers, abundant officials, and priests appeared, the middle one having on his back a
cross embroidered as long as his body. This
was the beginning of the sacramental service.
Then ensued such a scene of theatrical gym-
nastics, such a series of strange movements of
the priests, their backs almost always to the
people, as I never saw before even in a Romish
temple. Clouds upon clouds of incense, the
censer frequently refreshed by the high priest
who kissed the spoon as he dug out the sacred
powder, and swung it about at the end of a
silver chain. A quarter of an hour sufficed to
administer to about seventy communicants,

out of six hundred present. An hour and
three-quarters was given to the histrionic part.
The communicants went up to the tune of
soft music, as though it had been a melo-
drama, and one was astonished at the close
that there was no fall of the curtain. 'God is a
Spirit; and they that worship him must worship him in spirit and in truth.' "

He speaks of presiding at a meeting of the
London Missionary Society in aid of their
missions in China, and added sadly:

"I shall, I suppose, give great offense to my
friends in the Establishment. Am sorry for
it; but the cause is too holy, too catholic, too
deeply allied with the single name of Christ,
for any considerations of Church system and
Episcopal rule. What is the meaning of 'Grace
be with all those who love the Lord Jesus
Christ in sincerity?' Did not Morrison, Mof-
fatt, Williams, love him? If grace, then, was
with those men, shall I, vile man, presume to
say that I will not be with them also?"

He was thoroughly in sympathy with the

British and Foreign Bible Society. His interest was first made manifest at the time of the Great Exhibition in Hyde Park in 1851. The religious societies desired to make it the occasion, while so many foreigners were in the land, of pressing the claims of the gospel in various ways. Lord Shaftesbury tells of his efforts to obtain a place for the translation of the Bible:

"There was no difficulty whatever in obtaining abundant space for all the implements of war and of human destruction that the mind of man could imagine. A large proportion of the Exhibition was taken up with guns, cannons, torpedoes, everything that could annoy and desolate mankind. It was suggested that we should erect for the Bible Society some place in the Exhibition, where we could show proofs of all that we had done to the praise of God, and all we were capable of doing. Some said we had no right to appear. I had a long interview with His Royal Highness, the Prince Consort, on the subject, and he took

the view that the Bible Society had *no* right
to a position there. I said:

" 'Putting aside the religious aspect of the
question, I will put it before you from an intellectual point of view. I ask you whether it
is not a wonderful proof of intellectual power
that the Word of God has been translated into
one hundred and seventy distinct languages,
and into two hundred and thirty dialects? Is
it not a proof of great intellectual power that
the agents of the Bible Society have given a
written character to more than thirty distinct
languages, enabling all those people to read
the Word of God in their own tongue?'

"He said: 'You have proved your right to
appear. It is a great intellectual effort, and I
will do my best to secure for the Society such
a position as is befitting.' "

That year he took the chair for the first
time as president of the British and Foreign
Bible Society, a position which he held
through his long life. In moving a resolution
that the meeting should unite in expressing

their best wishes that the blessing of God should rest upon their new president, the Earl of Harrowby said:

"I am sure, my Lord, that you will not hold cheap the honor which has been conferred upon you. I conceive that it is the highest honor within the realm of England to be the representative of her religious principles and feelings; and I believe that there is not a man in the whole realm who enjoys the general approbation of his fellow-citizens more than your lordship. You have pursued your service for mankind, undeterred by difficulties, by opposition, by sneers; uninjured by popularity, uninfluenced by unpopularity. We are convinced that your conduct throughout has been based on the deepest personal religious convictions."

His biographer describes a great meeting of the Society near the close of Shaftesbury's life. It was at Exeter Hall, and on the occasion he made one of his famous orations on the Bible. It was an answer to the Neologists, who had been publishing a declaration that the Bible was effete.

"Multitudes are pressing in at the open doors of Exeter Hall. A group of foreigners on the opposite pavement are looking on in blank astonishment; they are gazing at a sight which is more characteristic of English life and feeling than can be seen at any other place, or at any other season. It is the festival time of England's great religious societies.

"Enter the building. It is thronged in every part. Presently the organ ceases to play, and there is a stir and a flutter in the audience as divines, philanthropists, and social and religious leaders take their position on the platform. But the signal for a spontaneous burst of enthusiastic greeting is given when the secretary precedes a tall, slender, pale-faced man, who gazes for a moment with cold, passionless eyes upon the sea of heads and the waving handkerchiefs as he holds the rail of the platform nervously, and then, after a formal bow, buries himself in the depths of a

16

huge arm-chair.   Every person in the hall claims to know and revere him.

"He rises to speak, and again the hall rings with repeated cheers.   He stands unmoved—still as a statue.   He seems unconscious that he is the object of attention.   As the cheering continues, he seems almost displeased with the demonstration, for no shadow of a smile passes over the strongly-marked lines of his face.   When the echoes of the thunderings have died away, he draws his slight form to its full height, grasps firmly the rail of the platform, and commences his speech.   It proceeds on a somewhat dead level, although uttered with great dignity until he alludes to certain philosophical works recently issued to teach that the Bible is unsuited to the present times.   Then the whole manner of the man is changed; the pale face kindles; the voice becomes clear and ringing; the slender form is all alive with strength and energy; the whole man is transfigured.   He marshals in swift array the nations of the world, and shows that the Bible has brought to them liberty and civilization and blessings untold. He closes with a peroration of wonderful power:

" 'They tell us that the Bible is effete. It is effete as Abraham was effete when he became the father of many nations, when there sprang of one, and him as good as dead, as many as the stars for multitude and the sands upon the seashore innumerable. It is effete as eternity. It is effete as God himself is effete, the same yesterday, to-day, and forever.' "

He enjoyed the close personal friendship of many famous men and women—the Duke of Wellington, Garibaldi, the Prince Consort, and Queen Victoria. A letter written to him from Daniel Webster just before Webster's appointment as Secretary of State, is interesting, as indicating the friendly feeling existing between the great American statesman and the English philanthropist:

"I owe you many thanks for a kind note which I received at the moment of my departure from London, and for the present of a copy of the Holy Bible. You could have given me nothing more acceptable, and I shall keep it near me as a valued token of your regard. The older I grow, and the more I read the Holy Scriptures, the more reverence I have for them, and the more convinced I am that they are not only the best guide for the conduct of this life, but the foundation of all hope respecting a future state of existence. I have an edition of the New Testament which I am fond of using. It is the authorized text, without being broken into verses.

"I read your speech on introducing your bill with great interest. Indeed, I read all you say, and notice all you do, with interest.

"I have the honor to be,

"Yours with faithful regard,

"DANIEL WEBSTER."

Charles Dickens was always a warm admirer of Shaftesbury. He sought an introduction to him, and on several occasions aided

his labors among the poor. He paid hearty
tribute to the good results of Lord Shaftesbury's philanthropic work. He described various wretched localities as he first knew them,
and as they were after Lord Shaftesbury had
established there a Ragged School or mission.

Lord Shaftesbury makes this most interesting note on Dickens, when he receives a
copy of Forster's "Life of Dickens:"

"The man was a phenomenon, an exception, a special production. Nothing like him
ever preceded. Nature is n't such a tautolo-
gist as to make another to follow him. He
was set, I doubt not, to rouse attention to
many evils and many woes; and though not
putting it on Christian principle (which would
have rendered it unacceptable), he may have
been in God's unfathomable goodness as much
a servant of the Most High as the pagan Naa-
man, 'by whom the Lord had given deliver-
ance to Syria!' God gave him, as I wrote to
Forster, a general retainer against all suffering and oppression."

Lord Shaftesbury was no less remarkable
for his friends in humble life, whom he grap-
pled to his soul with hooks of steel. He
seemed to know instinctively whom he could
trust, and having once given work into the
hands of a chosen helper, he inspired him with
his own mighty faith and courage.

He one day happened upon a man named
Roger Miller, who had gathered a hundred
destitute and forsaken children in a tumble-
down building, and was teaching them. He
brought him material aid, and entered him on
his list of friends. Miller was a frequent and
welcome visitor in Shaftesbury's home, and
Lord Shaftesbury declared that the city missionary was so full of practical piety and cheerful faith as to bring untold blessing with his
very presence. He died suddenly, and Lord
Shaftesbury recorded it thus:

"A far greater man might have gone out
of the world with much less effect. All was
grief on Monday at Broadwell. Children and
adults wept alike, and blessed the memory of

Roger Miller. I have known men of a hundred thousand a year depart this life, and every eye around dry as the pavement. Here goes a city missionary at thirty shillings a week, and hundreds are in an agony of sorrow. I have lost an intimate friend. We took 'sweet counsel together, and walked to the house of God as friends.' A gap has been made in my life and occupations which will not be easily filled up."

It made no difference to him what a man was in the eye of society or of the world, if he saw in him one who possessed those qualities upon which true friendship alone can rest. He esteemed a man first for what he was in himself, and next, for what he was doing for the world to make it brighter and happier and holier.

A prison philanthropist, Thomas Wright, was such a friend. In a talk to young men, Lord Shaftesbury said:

"Many of you must have heard of a remarkable man of Manchester named Thomas

Wright. He visited prisons. He was engaged all day long in a small establishment
acting as foreman, covered with oil and grease.
The first time I ever saw him I was stopping
in Manchester with my friend, the great engi-
neer, Mr. Fairbairn. He said to me:

"'You have heard of Thomas Wright;
would you like to meet him?'

"I said: 'Of course I should, beyond anything.'

"'Well, then, we shall have him to dinner.'

"So we asked him to dinner. He came,
and had I not known who he was, I should
have said he was the most venerable doctor of
divinity I ever looked upon. His hair was
white; his face was benignant and beautiful.
We passed the evening and went to Church
together. Two or three days afterward, we
said we would go and see Thomas Wright.
We knocked at the office door, and a man, in
a paper cap and an apron, and covered with
grease, opened it. I passed in, and I said: 'I
want to see Thomas Wright.' 'I dare say you

do,' he said; 'here I am.' Then I said: 'Bless
you, my good fellow, never was I so impressed
in my life before, as I am now with the true
dignity of labor.'

"When his work was over, he doffed his
cap, washed his face, put on his black clothes,
and away he went to prison, to carry life and
light and the gospel of Christ to many broken
and anxious hearts."

Never for one moment did his interest for
suffering childhood abate. As late as 1871 he
found abuses existing among the children employed in pottery and porcelain works. He
carried through legislation to give them relief.
He had already investigated and relieved child
labor in pin and needle factories, calico-print-
ing and button factories. Then he learned
that by a technical difficulty children employed in brickfields were excluded from the
benefits of the legislation. Lord Shaftesbury
could not rest until this injustice was set right.
He addressed the House of Lords, and stated
that there were in the country three thousand

brickyards, and that the number of children and young persons employed in them amounted to nearly thirty thousand, their ages varying from three and a half to seventeen. A large proportion of these were females, and the hours during which they were kept at their monstrous toil was from fourteen to sixteen per day.

His efforts were successful, and children in brickfields came under the beneficent protection of law.

He became interested in the wretched seamstresses of London. He prepared a bill for their protection and proper payment. As usual, there was great indifference in the House of Lords and with the press. He says:

"Not a paper, except the *Standard*, has uttered a word in defense of these poor, helpless, oppressed girls. Their sufferings are sad, cruel, overwhelming. How shall I prosper with my bill? All is in His hands, who cares as much for the smallest, sickliest seamstress as for all the grand ladies of the land."

His biographer gives us a graphic picture of Lord Shaftesbury's own personal service, which shows us how truly he was himself a missionary, how closely he followed his Master:

"In one of the most depraved quarters of London, in a neighborhood with a network of disreputable courts and alleys, the resort of notorious ill-doers, the dread of timid way-farers, and the despair of the police, there sit in an ill-furnished room two or three men, waiting anxiously. They are men belonging to humble but respectable walks of life, and have, it would seem, nothing in common with the people who pass along the street—the crop-headed jail-birds, the cunning-faced cadgers, the sickly, ill-clad women, hurrying away to creep into holes and corners for the night. The street grows quieter; the great clock of St. Paul's has some time since boomed out the hour of midnight. Presently there is heard the firm, steady tread of one who walks as with a purpose. The step is recognized; the door is thrown open, and the watchers grasp the hand of the stranger—a tall, slight, pale-faced man, with a grave and thoughtful expression of countenance.

"He returns the salutation cordially, although it is obvious that he belongs to a different rank from those with whom he is associated, and without delay proceeds to the business that has brought him to this strange place at this strange hour. A hurried conference is held, certain plans are discussed, there is a still and solemn silence for a few minutes, and then all the party rise, button up their stout overcoats, and sally forth, one of the number bearing in his hand a small parcel of candles!

"They walk in silence until they reach their destination—the Victoria Arches under Holborn Hill, known as the Vagrants' Hiding-place—where they light their candles, and enter the dark, dismal vaults. As they enter, a few poor, miserable, hunted wretches brush hastily past, and make their escape into the street, or plunge into the recesses of the hiding-place, conscience making cowards of them all.

"It is some time before the visitors can distinguish objects distinctly; the darkness is intense, and some of the arches are vast. As their eyes become more accustomed to the gloom, they see sights which can not now, thank God! be seen, and will never more be seen in the great city where vice and misery are rampant.

"There, spread on the dank floor, on layers of rotten straw, filled with vermin of all kinds, lie wretched human beings, whose poverty or wrong-doing has deprived them of every other resting-place.

"As the light falls upon their faces, some of them start up with the keen, cunning look of those who know that they have broken the laws, and must depend upon their wits to escape the penalty; others turn over with a sigh of weariness, and draw around them the scanty garments that scarcely cover them;

while others break out into foul imprecations upon the intruders.

"Everywhere, in holes and corners, some almost burrowing into the soil, others lying closely side by side for the sake of warmth, are to be seen these poor outcasts, sheltering in the only place where they can rest. Terrible are the faces that meet the gaze of the visitors, faces that bear indelible marks made by vice, disease, or sorrow; faces that haunt the imagination long afterwards.

"Not to gaze and moralize, but to work, is the object of the visitors; not to pity only, but to help. And by two o'clock in the morning they have taken thirty of these wretched outcasts, and have brought them from the cold and darkness of the arches into the light and warmth of a comparatively cheerful room used as a Ragged School. Among the rescued are two boys, mere skin and bone in bundles of rags, whose sunken jaws and sparkling eyes tell the story of their sickness, and want, and premature decay. They are seated on either side of the tall, slight man, whose sorrowful eyes have grown more sorrowful as he looks upon them through the mist of his tears. They are brothers in affliction, who have been drawn together by mutual need, for both are orphans. One of them remembers a home; but when his father died he was left friendless and destitute, and in his misery found a shelter in the dark arches, where his companion had slept alone every night for a whole year, until this companion in misfortune came to share the straw and the rags that made his bed.

"But the dawning of this day has brought with it the dawning of hope. The 'kind gentleman,' beside whom they sit, has spoken to them words of tenderness and pity. And when they learn from him that they need no more go back to the arches, but may find comfort and help and home in a Refuge for the Homeless, their hearts, grown hard and cold with the world's neglect, are opened, and they weep for very joy.

"As their rescuer returned towards his home that morning, his head was bowed and his heart was heavy. He knew that there were hundreds, and it might be thousands, of boys in the great city in as hopeless a case, who were drifting from bad to worse until they should be past hope; and he knew not how they were to be reached. By day and night the wailing of the world's sorrow haunted him. The cry of the children rang ceaselessly in his ears. And it was no figure of speech he used, when those who saw his cheeks grow paler, and his face more sad, asked him of the cause, and he answered with choking voice:

" 'I have been in a perfect agony of mind about my poor boys!' "

He was several times invited to meet with companies of thieves, that he might help them into honest employment. After such a meeting, he said:

"Last night I met with thirty thieves. What a spectacle! what misery! what degradation! and yet I question whether we, fine, easy, comfortable folks, are not greater sinners in the sight of God than are these poor wretches."

When visiting the Day Ragged School, which he frequently did, he would go the round of each section, notice their lessons, and encourage them to persevere. One winter's day, speaking to a poor boy with a pallid face, he asked, "My man, what's the matter with you?" The boy replied, "I have had no food for some time." "How long have you been without?" "About twenty-six hours." "Twenty-six hours!" said the Earl; "no wonder you look ill."

He questioned the scholars, and found that many of them were half-starved. He turned and left the room, saying, while the tears rained down his face, "Poor, dear children!"

He stepped into his carriage, and ordered his coachman to drive home. A few hours after, large churns of soup were sent down, enough to feed four hundred. This continued, and that winter ten thousand basins of soup

17

and bread were distributed to hungry children—soup made in his own mansion at Grosvenor Square.

In 1866, Lord Shaftesbury inaugurated a
movement which he had been considering for
several years. He sent invitations to the
casual wards and to similar places of resort,
inviting some of the homeless boys of London, under sixteen years of age, to a supper
at St. Giles Refuge.

It was a cold, wet night, and when the one
hundred and fifty who had given in their
names made their appearance, they presented
a miserable spectacle. Their garments were
tattered and torn, and were hanging about
their limbs, rather than covering them. The
majority were barefooted, and all of them belonged to the most forlorn and wretched
classes of society.

On being questioned, they gave ready answers concerning their miserable history.
Most of them begged for a livelihood, and

slept at night in casual wards or refuges, and knew nothing whatever of their parents. After a good supper an adjournment was made to another room, where a kind of conference was held as to any means that might be devised for rescuing boys of this class from the career of crime and misery which awaited them.

Lord Shaftesbury asked a series of direct questions. He said first:

"Let all those boys who have ever been in prison, hold up their hands."

Immediately about thirty hands went up.

"Let those who have been in prison twice, hold up their hands."

Ten hands went up.

"How many in prison three times?"

Five hands appeared.

"Is it the case that most of you boys are running about town all day, and sleeping where you can at night?"

There was a unanimous "Yes!"

"How do you get your livelihood?"

Some boys called out, "Holding horses," "Begging," "Cleaning boots."

"Would you like to get out of your present line of life, and into one of honest industry?"

The reply was a loud and enthusiastic "Yes!"

"Supposing that there were in the Thames a big ship, large enough to contain a thousand boys, would you like to be placed on board to be taught trades, or trained for the navy and merchant service?"

There was a forest of upraised hands and cries of "Yes."

"Do you think that another two hundred boys out of the street would say the same?"

"We do."

The boys were dismissed with kindly words; but a happy thought was set in motion that day. The *Times* took up the movement with great earnestness.

Two projects were at once discussed and approved. The first, to ascertain if the Lords of the Admiralty would give one of the useless ships of war, then lying in Her Majesty's dockyards, to be fitted up as a training-ship for homeless boys who would wish to follow a seafaring life.

The second was to obtain, by hire or gift, an old-fashioned house with about fifty acres of land, a few miles from London, where those boys not fitted for sea could be trained to agricultural pursuits, so as to supply the labor market at home, or to qualify themselves for colonial life.

The Government at once granted the *Chichester*, a fifty-gun frigate, which had never been out of dock.

Lord Shaftesbury went to see the ship in preparation for the school. He said:

"This has been a dream of fifteen years and more. We have dashed on, and are ready for action. If the means are supplied, the result is as certain as the movement of the planets; but I tremble lest the zeal of my friend Williams and my own may not have plunged us into responsibilities beyond our reach. God alone can give us of the nation's abundance, and make the rich pour their bounties into the treasury."

The movement proved to be in every way successful.

At the inauguration of the *Chichester*, Lord Shaftesbury said:

"Was it not a scandal that this great country, whose sole defense, under God, rested in her navy, could not man her ships, and had to depend, in a large degree, upon foreigners? It seems absolutely necessary that everything possible should be done to keep up the marine, and I believe, if the public support the present movement so that we might keep four hundred boys on board, we might every year send forth two hundred lads to navy service."

In course of time the *Arethusa* was granted for the same purpose. Later, a ship was built, and named the *Shaftesbury*. Lord Shaftesbury visited it frequently, and instituted a system of prizes for good behavior. Whenever he went he held a religious service, and gave them a talk so full of kind wishes and hope as to inspire the most hopeless fellow there to do his best, and bring honor and success to the movement.

The other division, the training for agricultural pursuits, was just as successful.

Several National Refuges for Homeless and Destitute Children were established. Two Girls' Refuges were opened at Sudbury and Ealing. Two large schools, one of them named the Shaftesbury, were founded to train boys for colonial life. And all of these organizations, which sprang from his busy brain and loving heart, have been through the years a blessing and an honor to the country.

Chapter XIII

IT was said that every London shoeblack knew Lord Shaftesbury, and felt that he was a personal friend. One day an acquaintance of his lordship's was having his boots cleaned, and he said to the lad,

"I've seen Lord Shaftsbury."

"Have you, indeed?" answered the boy; "I shall see him myself at our annual meeting of shoeblacks on Friday at Exeter Hall."

A public man, anxious to find out what was the real feeling of these Ragged School shoeblacks for their patron, spoke disparagingly of Lord Shaftesbury to one of them, and denounced him for assisting juvenile thieves and roughs, all of whom, he said, ought to be in prison, rather than at school. The poor boy was at once very indignant, and, with an angry voice and blazing cheeks, he cried out: "Do n't you speak against Lord Shaftesbury, sir; if you do, God Almighty will never bless you."

His oft-repeated declaration was, "What the poor want is not patronage, but sympathy." The poor saw him driving into their slums with his carriage full of toys for the neglected little ones. The great day of the year, the day spent in the country, they saw him moving about among them, with a kind word here, a little pleasantry there, and a smile for all. In their times of sickness he sat by their bedsides, and read to them from the Scriptures. When he promised to see them again, or send them books or comforts, *he was never known to leave one promise unfulfilled*, notwithstanding the many he made. He found tools for one to get employment, and advanced money to another till his first wages fell due.

They knew that if a poor flower-girl, or little children in distress, called at Grosvenor Square to tell their troubles to "the good Earl," they would never be turned away.

They knew that, by day and by night, he went to the common lodging-houses, and sought out men and women tenderly reared, who were hiding away from family and friends, and would not give up a case until he had seen them reconciled, and, perchance, brought home again.

The bare walls of those miserable lodging-houses on the day after his visit were found adorned with bright pictures, to produce the semblance of a homelike look.

When some of them told him of cruel wrong or heart-breaking sorrow, they saw the tears pour down his face, and heard his faltering exclamation, "God help you, poor dear!" It is no wonder that the common people loved him, and that his name was held in veneration in every hovel of Whitechapel and Westminster.

At a large gathering of costermongers, laborers, and common people, held in Westminster, a gentleman was anxious to test what knowledge people of this class had of great public men. He referred to one who, though well advanced in life, and pressed with a thousand engagements, could yet find time to write hymns in Latin, and translate them into Italian; but there was no recognition of the person from the description. Half a dozen of the leading men of the day were referred to in a similar manner without recognition from the audience.

But when the speaker only hinted at "the labors of one who is revered in the factory districts as the friend of the poor and the oppressed," there was immediately a loud clapping of hands; and when the speaker, to make sure that they understood, asked them, "I suppose, by that applause, you know to whom I refer?" there was a ready response, "Lord Shaftesbury."

Another gentleman, in another place, having indirectly referred to the work of Lord Shaftesbury without mentioning his name, was surprised to find himself interrupted by a storm of applause. He was sure the applause was not for what he had said, but for the man of whom he had spoken. Pausing in his address, he said :

"And what do you know of Lord Shaftesbury?"

"Know of him!" answered a man standing up in the audience; "why, sir, I'm a sweep, and what did he do for me? Did n't he pass the bill? When I was a little 'un, I had to go up the chimbleys, and many a time I've come down with bleeding feet and knees, and a'most choking. And he passed the bill as saved us from all that. That's what I know of him."

If the poor had many memorials of Lord Shaftesbury, he certainly had many of them. Over his bed in Grosvenor Square hung a handsome "sampler," worked by factory girls, the first-fruits of their leisure hours. The clock in his dining-room was presented to him by flower and watercress girls. His bed coverlet, under which at St. Giles he always slept, was made out of little bits of material, with a figure in the middle, and a large letter "S," the work of a company of ragged children.

Speaking one day at the Annual Meeting of the Reformatory and Refuge Union, he tried to tell how much he was indebted to these children, and said:

"I believe I have been pretty well clothed by day and night because of their service; I have had all sorts of things made and given to me; I have had slippers and stockings; I have had shoes and waistcoats and bed linen, coverlets, counterpanes—well, everything but a coat; I have had desks and arm-chairs and a quantity of writing-paper, all well stamped, sufficient for six months' correspondence. I love these gifts, because they have been called forth from the dear little hearts of these children, and so they are more precious than the noblest present could be.

"I thank God for the day when I was called by his grace to participate in this holy work. Of all the things to which I have been called by his good and all-wise providence, there is not one like it, not one that has brought me so much comfort, not one that I can look back upon with so much consolation, and there is not one that I look forward to with so much hope."

We should expect him to be kind and thoughtful towards the servants of his household; and so he was.

When speaking on behalf of an institution in which he took a great interest, the Aged Pilgrims' Friend Society, he was able to refer to the fact that his housekeeper had been fifty-two years in his service; that as nurse she had brought up all his children; that not one of them would ever think of retiring to rest in his house without bidding "good night" to that "female patriarch," and that she was held in reverence by all the household.

He did not say, what was nevertheless the fact, that every morning after prayers it was his habit to shake hands with the aged housekeeper, and inquire after her health, and of things that were of interest in her little world.

Many who had bitterly opposed his work in his earlier years, became his warm admirers in the later part of his life. A great dinner was given by a society of noble rank, to celebrate the admission of Lord Hartington, who made a speech on the occasion. He said:

"I find upon the roll the names of Lord Grey, Lord John Russell, Lord Holland, and Mr. Hume; and coming down a little later, I find the names of Lord Palmerston, Lord Clarendon, and Mr. Cobden; and descending to our own time, I find the name of Mr. Gladstone; and last upon the roll, I find the name of one who has been admitted, not for political services, but for services purer, nobler, and more illustrious than any which we politicians can hope to render; I mean that of my noble friend who sits beside me—Lord Shaftesbury."

Lord Shaftesbury speaks of the occasion thus:

"There was one little episode that greatly pleased me. It came from Lord Hartington, the hero of the evening, as we had met to honor his admission to the freedom of the company. I did not expect it. I did not know that he cared anything for me personally, or had watched my career."

His humility helps us to understand how great he was. On his seventieth birthday he wrote:

"I have been thinking of my past career and present position; and am astonished how I went through one, and now stand in the other. I am without pretense to literary attainments, though with an immense fondness for them. I am intellectually not strong; a poor and ineffective orator, though foolishly desirous of being a great one. Yet I have had successes, great successes. How were they attained? I know not. The only qualities I can claim for myself are feeling, conviction, and perseverance. These have, under God, brought me to the position I now hold. What is my stock-in-trade for the duties of the next session? So far as I can estimate, they are remnants of intellectual power, remnants of influence, remnants of doings considered as past services, remnants of zeal, all backed by a certain amount of public forbearance."

At an evening party given by Sir Henry Rawlinson to the members of the Arctic Expedition, at which Lord Shaftesbury was present, Sir Bartle Frere took the opportunity to urge upon him that he should visit the United States. Referring to this, he says:

"It is what I had long and often wished; but as St. Paul says, 'Was let hitherto.' Now I am too near the sensible decay of physical and mental power for such an effort as that would be. The demands on my strength in every form would far surpass what I could have endured, even in my younger days."

At another time he said concerning our country:

"The United States are a young country; and so far as an analogy is good, have all the hopes and prospects of healthy and vigorous youth. They contain within themselves every-

18

thing, however various, that nature bestows, and in abundance inexhaustible. In art and science, they are equal to the best; in energy of character, superior. They have nothing to fear from internal dissensions; they are beyond the power of foreign aggression. Their territory is nearly boundless, and so close as to furnish a ready safety-valve to all their discontented spirits. Every year adds enormously to their numbers and resources, and wealth seems to grow like the grass of the field.

"The Government is essentially republican; and there is actually nothing left to contend for in the way of more liberal institutions. They may, and will, have party strifes and struggles for the possession of place and power; but what social question remains? There is no State Church to be invaded; no aristocracy to be pulled down; no king to be replaced by a President."

The evening-time of his life found him laboring on, his faculties keenly alive, his heart tender as ever, his sympathies just as fresh, and his plans as numerous as at any period of his life. He prayed, "O Lord, let me die in the harness!"

Lord Shaftesbury's eightieth birthday was celebrated as a national event. Under the auspices of the Lord Mayor, the committee of the Ragged School Union took the initiative to do honor to their president, and a great meeting in the Guild Hall was arranged to celebrate the day, and to present him with a portrait of himself. It was a famous gathering. Long before the commencement of the proceedings, every part of the great building was crowded. On the platform was assembled a distinguished company, including members of both Houses of Parliament, clergymen, merchant princes, men and women representing every estimable phase of political, religious, and social life, to do honor to the man who had proved himself the greatest benefactor of his generation. It was a brilliant assembly.

But even more suggestive was the scene outside the building, where flower-girls with their well-filled baskets of spring flowers, and costermongers with their gayly-dressed donkeys and barrows, and Ragged School children, crowded around the hero of the day, scattering flowers in his path, and pouring upon him "the blessing of the poor, and of him that was ready to perish."

The Earl of Aberdeen, Mr. W. E. Forster, and the Lord Mayor were the principal speakers. When Lord Shaftesbury arose to reply to the addresses, he was greeted with a perfect tempest of applause. He was calm and self-possessed, and amid all the excitement and fatigue he did not omit one point of interest in his career, nor did he forget to render tributes of gratitude to the many who had supported him in his lifelong labors.

There were many incidents in that magnificent celebration which affected him, but nothing more than the manly and generous speech of Mr. W. E. Forster. He valued it, not because of Mr. Forster's high official position, but because he was a mill-owner in Yorkshire who knew the evils which had existed in the factory districts, and who had been one of the first to speak a kind word to him on his earliest visit to the town of Bradford. There was one expression in the speech which particularly gratified Lord Shaftesbury, and he said afterward:

"If anything is told of my life after I am gone, let those words of Forster's be recorded. In the whole course of my life, no words have gratified me more."

These were the words:

"The good conduct on the part of the population was, in a great measure, due to the moderating influences which were brought to bear on them by Lord Shaftesbury. How I wish that all agitators, when they are advocating the removal of great and real grievances, would take an example from him, and

remember with what care they should consider both the immediate and the ultimate
effect of what they say upon those who are
suffering."

All the doings of that day were issued in
book form by the committee of the Ragged
School Union, a special copy of which was
presented to Lord Shaftesbury. On the fly-
leaf he wrote:

"Deep and lively is my gratitude to the
men who conceived, organized, and executed
this celebration, and much do I feel the sympathy of those who honored it by their presence."

Letters of congratulation poured in from
all the great men and women of England; tele-
grams flashed and presents were unloaded at
his door.

But the gift which he most highly prized
was a bouquet of paper flowers, made and
presented by the little children of the One Tun
Ragged School.

He received this beautiful message from his sister:

"I have thought much of you to-day, you dear, blessed darling. May God continue to watch over your most precious life!

"Your devoted sister, CHARLOTTE."

Every day brought its labors—meetings, speeches, interviews, letters involving deliberation and wise action. He was eighty-two years old when he made his great speech at the Luther Commemoration. It was a magnificent eulogium of "a man chosen by God himself, to deliver us from the most terrible and degrading thralldom of mind and spirit that ever fell upon the human race."

The same day he laid the foundation-stone of a place of worship at Whitechapel, and attended a great meeting in the evening, where he presided. He said:

"I got through it all without pain or fatigue. Speeches, of course, at each. I bless

Thee, O Lord! He can, and he does, often-
times make an iron pillar out of a bulrush."

Large sums of money came into his hands
every year for the support of his great enter-
prises. A few months before his death, he
received the astonishing announcement that
a lady had left to him in her will for distribution among the charities of London the sum
of sixty thousand pounds! The toil and anxiety consequent upon the disposal of this large
sum can be understood only by those who
knew how scrupulously conscientious Lord
Shaftesbury was in dealing with every farthing of money of which he was trustee.

May of 1885 came, and brought the great
religious festivals of the year. It was his
earnest desire that he might be able to preside at the Bible Society meeting and at the
Ragged School Union.

His friends did not see how it was possible
for him to bear the fatigue and excitement
attendant upon these great gatherings; but he

was there. And his voice rang out as clear and strong as of yore. He was also able to get to the anniversary of the Flower Girls' Mission.

He made two important speeches, one on behalf of Ragged Schools, at Grosvenor House; and one at Mansion House, for the protection of helpless women and girls from dangers in the streets. When he saw that he had not strength to carry this measure through and secure legislation, he was quite heartbroken. He said to a friend:

"I feel old age creeping on, and know I must soon die. I hope it is not wrong to say it—but *I can not bear to leave this world with all the misery in it.*"

It gave him great joy to install as superintendent of a school a fine young tradesman who had been a wretched little vagrant, but, educated in the Ragged School, had become fitted for the position.

He made his last visit to these schools,

which had been his thought and care for so many years. A superintendent writes:

"I shall never forget that visit. He went the round of the rooms, interested in the poor children and people as much as ever, speaking tenderly and sympathizingly to sorrowing · ones, and telling them of Jesus, an ever-loving and ever-present Savior. Then he said:

" 'I do n't think I shall ever see you in the flesh again. I am ill, and at my time of life I can not expect to be long here. What a comfort it is to know Christ as a personal Savior;' and, after a pause, he added, 'My Savior.' "

His physicians decided that he must get away from the excitement of London life for a time at least. He left London, July 25th, for the last time, and went to Folkstone, where he could drink in the invigorating sea-air.

Very sacred grew that chamber where the prayer was constantly breathed, "Come, Lord Jesus, come quickly." He would ask his daughters or his valet to read to him portions of the Bible he named to them. Every morn-

ing he called for the twenty-third Psalm, beginning, "The Lord is my Shepherd: I shall
not want."

His only regret was that he could not die
in his own home.

When a letter from the Dean of Westminster was read to him, in which a resting-place
in Westminster Abbey was proposed, he said
in an earnest voice, "No—St. Giles's!"

His sons and daughters, whom he had
loved with an untold affection, knelt for his
benediction. He said to them with a restful
smile:

"I am in the hands of God, the ever-blessed
Jehovah; in his hands alone. Yes, in his keep-
ing, with him alone."

The first day of October, when the sunshine, which he loved so much, was flooding
his chamber with light, he passed, without
pain or sigh, into the presence of the King.

A week later, as simple a funeral procession
as ever marked the public obsequies of a great
man moved away from the door of his house

in Grosvenor Square. It needed not the pomp of any earthly pageant to do him honor. Flowers sent by poor and rich alike formed the only display. There were signs of mourning in the clubhouses and mansions of St. James Street and Pall Mall; but it was far more significant to see the thousands of artisans, laborers, factory hands, flower-girls, the poor and destitute from all quarters of London, lining the streets through which the procession was to pass.

Even the poorest had managed to procure some little fragment of black to wear upon the coat-sleeve or in the bonnet. The stillness was solemn and impressive. And as the simple procession passed, every head was uncovered and bowed as with a personal sorrow. He had "clothed a people with spontaneous mourning, and was going down to the grave amid the benedictions of the poor." His biographer says:

"As the funeral carriages passed into Parliament Street, a sight was seen which will

never be forgotten while this generation lasts.
Deputations from the Homes and Refuges
and training-ships, from the costermongers'
society, from missions and charities, each with
their craped banners emblazoned with such
words as these, 'Naked, and ye clothed me,'
'A stranger, and ye took me in.' As the procession passed, the deputations fell in, and
marched towards the Abbey.

"Rarely, if ever, had there been such a company assembled in Westminster Abbey as on
that day.   Royalty was represented; the
Church, both Houses of Parliament, diplomacy, municipal power, society, were represented.   But the real importance of that enormous gathering, filling every inch of space,
lay in the spontaneous homage of the thousands of men and women representing all that
was powerful for good in the whole land.   The
Abbey was full of mourners.   Never before in
the memory of living men had there been
brought together, at one time, in one place,
and with one accord, so many workers for the

common good, impelled by a deep and tender sympathy in a common loss. For no other man in England, or in the world, could such an assembly have been brought together."

After the burial service, with its sweet words of Christian joy and the strong words of Christian confidence, that vast congregation joined in singing Charles Wesley's hymn:

"Let all the saints terrestrial sing
With those to glory gone,
For all the servants of our King,
In earth and heaven, are one."

The coffin was buried beneath masses of exquisite wreaths—the offering of the Crown Princess of Germany resting beside the "Loving tribute from the Flower-girls of London."

As the procession moved from the Abbey, the band of the Costermongers' Society played the hymn, "Safe in the arms of Jesus." A poor laboring man, with a piece of crape sewed on to his sleeve, turned to one who stood beside him, and, with a choking voice, said: "Our Earl's gone! God A'mighty knows he loved us, and we loved him. We shall not see his likes again!"

Ten thousand such tributes as this were paid that day to this English nobleman, whose nobility was less that of the garter and the escutcheon than of the Christian and the universal benefactor.

Next day, in the little church of St. Giles, the "good Earl" was laid to rest in the ancestral burying-place, beside the faithful wife and daughters whom he had loved so tenderly. This beautiful hymn closed the simple service:

> "Now the laborer's task is o'er,
>   Now the battle-day is past;
> Now upon the farther shore
>   Lands the voyager at last.
> Father, in thy gracious keeping
> Leave me now, thy servant sleeping."

A plain tablet has since been placed in the village church where he sleeps. He directed

that there should be nothing but a little tablet,
and chose the Scripture verses for it:

ANTONY ASHLEY COOPER,
Seventh Earl of Shaftesbury.
Born, April 28, 1801.
Died, October 1, 1885.

"What hast thou, that thou didst not receive?"
"Let him that thinketh he standeth, take heed lest
he fall."
"Surely, I come quickly. Even so, come, Lord
Jesus."

When, in 1885, the Duke of Argyll said,
"The social reforms of the last century have
been due to the influence, character, and perseverance of one man—Lord Shaftesbury,"
Lord Salisbury indorsed this eloquent tribute,
by adding, "That is, I believe, a very true representation of the facts."

While those who thronged the Abbey that
sad day shed their tears, ten thousand times
ten thousand of operatives, whose labor he had
lightened, of orphans he had sheltered, of outcasts he had rescued, of the oppressed he had
set free, of ragged children he had clothed, of

emigrants he had transplanted to new spheres, of Christian laborers whose zeal he had increased, paused in their daily tasks to share in the expression of universal grief.

The statute-books showed that his service had benefited a population of two million and five hundred persons!

He was the founder of a new order of nobility—an order of men who, inspired by his beautiful example, and catching his sublime enthusiasm for the lessening of human suffering and for the salvation of humankind, are bringing in the kingdom of our Lord and Savior, Jesus Christ.

Is it too much to say that he was the greatest man England has ever produced?

19